THE MOONLIGHT SERIES

THE HARVEST MOON

A PREQUEL

BY CHANEL HARDY

Hardy Publications

chardypublications.com

Thank you to my readers who loved these characters as much as I did.

-Chanel

The Harvest Moon

PROLOGUE

January 2014

"Thanks for asking me out, the movie was nice." A young woman said, clinging to the arm of Bryce Barbeau. "So, what now?" She asked as they exited the theatre.

Bryce looked at her, pausing their step. He wore a blank expression, sizing her up with his hooded eyes. He pressed his thumb against her cheek, caressing her face. His lips turned slightly upwards in a smirk.

"I wanna show you something." He said in a low voice.

The sky turned a scarlet shade as the sun began making its way below the horizon. Just as Bryce pulled up to a vacant lot on the outskirts of town. The girl stuck her head out of the passenger's side window, looking at the emptiness around them.

"Where are we?" She asked.

"It's a surprise." He said, turning off the engine. "You like surprises, don't you?"

"Yeah, of course." She chuckled faintly, fiddling with the hem of her dress.

He got out of the car, and she followed behind as he led her down a hill. At the bottom of the hill, was a stone structure that sat halfway buried in high grass. Bryce pulled open the metal door, with the girl not far behind. As he held the door open for her, she stopped, rubbing her forearms as goosebumps formed.

"What is this place?" She asked.

"It's my little secret. My parents live with me, so no privacy at home. You know how it is." He said, extending his hand to her.

"Right," She gave a soft giggle, still apprehensive but taking his hand anyway.

When Bryce Barbeau asked you out, you didn't decline. He was the most sought after young bachelor in all of Marksville. He had money, and his family name carried weight around the entire county of Avoyelles Parish. As he led her inside the damp, dark space, there was another door. This door was made of stone with no handle. He pressed his palm against it, whispering something under his breath as the door opened, leading to stairs. The girl was too busy swatting at gnats and pinching her nose because of the moldy smell she didn't even notice what he was doing. He pulled her along, his grip getting tighter as he picked up his pace once the door closed behind them. Once they got to the bottom, the area was dark but lit with candles everywhere.

"How romantic." The girl said, unconvincingly.

He turned, facing her and placing his hands on her shoulders. His hands made their way up, caressing the sides of her neck. The glare from candlelight shined across his face, broadcasting his features. His green eyes, sinister like. The girl's heart began to beat rapidly.

"Don't be scared." He said. "I'm not going to hurt you." He grinned widely, leaning in and kissing her on the lips.

Someone came up behind her, grabbing her arms and pulling her away. She screamed, trying to break free as they grabbed her wrists, slamming her against a wall as they cuffed her to a set of chains.

Bryce wiped his mouth, reaching into his pocket and pulling out a blade. "Jesus Christ, I'm so ready to be done with this." He huffed, relaxing his shoulders.

"We almost didn't make it in time." The boy said. "The full moon is almost out."

"Well, what do you want me to do?" Said Bryce. "They have to come at their own free will. I don't make the rules. Let's just get this over with.".

"Please don't hurt me!" The girl cried, her face wet with tears.

Bryce drew closer, "I said I wasn't going to hurt you, remember?" He handed his blade to the other boy. "But he is."

The girl's eyes grew wide as the boy lodged the blade into her chest. Impaling her in the heart. A scream emerged, getting caught in her throat as she choked on the blood filling her lungs, the boy held a cup over the gushing wound, catching the blood as it fell. The girl's chest heaved as she let out one last whimper before life completely vanished from her eyes.

He handed the cup to Bryce, who swirled it under his nose, inhaling the fleshy aroma as he took a sip of her warm blood. A crooked grin formed on his thin lips. He looked at the girl's dead body, gushing with blood and hanging from the chains.

Two down, one to go...

CHAPTER 1

Three weeks later…

"Oh my god, look how thick your hair was!" Kayla exclaimed, shoving the photo in Jackson's face.

Her braids hung over his shoulder as she sat behind him on the bed. She placed a soft peck on his cheek.

He got up, grabbing the photo from her, and looking at it with a smirk. She was right, his hair was a mess back then. It was a photo of him, Kayla, and her brother Leon when they were eleven, on a fishing trip. He placed the photo back on the bed and walked over to his dresser to finish packing his things. Kayla picked up the photo, getting off the bed, and walking over to him.

"Aren't you going to take it with you?" She asks, with the photo outstretched in her hands.

"No, I think you should keep it." He tells her, pushing her hand away gently.

Kayla stands there, holding the photo against her chest. "So that's it huh. I guess you don't want to remember us." She placed the photo on the dresser behind him.

Jackson places his hand on her shoulder. "Come on, you know it's not like that."

She looked down at the floor. He lifted her chin as they stared at each other, Kayla trying to hide her pain.

"Besides, you know where my dad's cabin is." He said.

"That's not the point." She said. "We're a pack. We're supposed to stay together."

"And we will. I'll always care about you guys. You know that. But that doesn't mean I have to stay in this house forever. I want to be on my own. I want to travel, see the world. Experience life outside of the shifter community in this city."

Kayla rolled her eyes. "Of course you do." She reached up to his face, placing her hands on the sides, gently stroking the hair above his ear with her thumbs. "You've always been the odd one out of all of us. It's the one thing I've never liked about you having fey blood. It makes you a little too human-like sometimes."

She leaned into him, pressing her lips against his. He kissed her back, giving her the satisfaction of this last moment of intimacy that they would ever share. He knew Kayla was right. He wasn't like the rest of them. While Leon, Kayla, and their father Hank were born from two purebred parents, Jackson was not. His father Silas was born from pure parents, but his mother Carla was a fey. A human turned shifter after a scratch or bite. Shifters like Jackson were still considered pure-born, but the bits of humanity from his mother still lingered within him.

He broke their embrace, pushing her hands away.

"Before I go, I want to make sure that you understand, where we are right now." He said.

"I don't need to be reminded, Jackson." She said with her arms crossed.

Letting out a slight huff.

"You and I... we were never going to be what you wanted us to be. We couldn't."

"I know. You made that clear three months ago." She said.

"I just don't want to leave here with you hating me."

Her eyes became glossy, she shrugged. "Can't make any promises."

He picked up his bag, tossing the straps of the duffle bag over his shoulder. "Goodbye, Kayla."

He walked out of the room, not looking back as she stood there, still with her arms crossed. Angry, bitter, and heartbroken.

He walked down the stairs, trying to quietly make his way to the door. As he touched the doorknob, his hand went cold.

"Leaving so soon," A voice uttered from the dining room.

Jackson let go of the knob, his hand forming into a grip. He turned, and slowly headed for the dining room. At the edge of the long, marble table, sat Hank. It was dark, and all Jackson could see was the figure hiding behind a huge puff of smoke as he stood at the opposite end.

"I thought you were sleeping," Jackson said. "I was just stopping by one last time to get the rest of my things."

"It's rude to leave your family without a goodbye. I know I taught you better than that." Hank leaned forward as the smoke cleared.

"My apologies sir. Well, this is goodbye I guess."

There was an uncomfortable silence, just the sound of Hank sliding his glass ashtray closer to him.

"No matter where you run off to, you can't escape who you are. And who you are meant to be." Hank said.

"We'll see about that." Jackson adjusted the straps of his bag on his shoulder, turned around, and headed back for the door. As he turned the knob to open the door, Hank called out to him one more time.

"We'll always be your family, Jackson," Hank said from the dining room. "You'll be back."

Jackson didn't respond. He headed out, getting inside the parked cab that awaited him.

***

Jackson arrived at this father's cabin, an American rosewood-stained log cabin built in the '80s. It was supposed to be his home. His family's home. But life had different plans. He didn't know much of his parents except for how they died. A hunting accident killed his father before he was born, and childbirth took his mother.

Hank never talked about Jackson's parents and seemed to avoid Jacksons questions about them whenever he had any. When Jackson asked him about having any other family, he simply said no. Followed with that look that meant to stop asking questions. But that wasn't the type of child Jackson was. He was curious and would stop at nothing to find out anything he could about his past.

He went inside and tossed his bag on the small sofa, heading to the bedroom. Pushing the bed away from the wall, he used his pocket knife to open the slits of the square cut into the wall. Pulling away the drywall, he reached inside the hole pulling out a box. In this box, he kept printouts of photos, and papers with information scribbled on them. He pulled out one of the photos, a picture of his mother. Carla Lakota.

Her long dark brown hair, tanned skin, and prominent but soft cheekbones, he saw himself in her. They also shared small, matching birthmarks. On their upper right arms. The man in the photo with his mother had one too. It must've run in the family. Of course, everyone always said he had his father's eyes. It was a photo taken of her as a teenager, with a man he assumed to be his grandfather. Jackson only saw one photo of his own father Silas. Hank kept it in the attic.

Being a shifter, he knew there would be no records of Silas. But after spending weeks online at the library, looking for records of women with his mother's name, born in the late 70s, he was coming up short. That's when he had the idea to search death certificates instead. Women named Carla who died on November 22, 1997, His birthday. He was able to track down one living relative on his mother's side. Carrie Lakota. She lived in Marksville, or at least that's what the records said. But they were from 2007. He wasn't even sure if she still lived at the address he found, but he had nothing to lose by finding out.

CHAPTER 2

After a ten-hour trip in a barley functioning station wagon, that he was able to purchase from a junkyard for cheap, Jackson finally arrived in Marksville, Louisiana. The only other time he left Illinois was when he was a kid. A trip to Missouri with Hank that he would rather forget. The humid air hugged his skin like a warm, moist blanket. Even in 75-degree weather, sweating was unavoidable. The GPS guided him down dusty roads where there seemed to be more trees than homes.

Turn left. The destination is on your right.

There it was. 2245 Elderberry drive. He turned off the car, grabbed the paper the address was written on from his pocket, looking over at the house, and back at the paper again. His stomach clenched as he bawled up the paper, tossing it on the passenger seat. Part of him wanted to start the engine and drive off. This seemed like a much better idea in his mind, and now that he was here, it felt like a huge mistake. But it was too late to turn back now. He got out of the car and walked up to the small, white, and blue bungalow home of Carrie Lakota. He inhaled and exhaled deeply, giving the door three knocks. He waited a few seconds before giving it another three knocks.

See, this was stupid. Way to go Jackson...

He looked over at the window near the door and saw a face peek through the pink curtains. He could hear the locks unlatching, and the door opened slightly. A woman stuck her head out the door.

"Can I help you?" She asked in a reluctant tone.

"Hello, ma'am." He greeted. My name is Jackson Kinnard. I'm looking for a woman named Carrie. Carrie Lakota."

The woman gazed him up and down. "I'm Carrie. What's your business with me?" She asked.

"You had a sister, named Carla. Right?"

She opened the door wider, getting a better look at him. Standing just a few inches shorter than him, she was a spitting image of the photos he saw of his mother.

"Why are you asking about Carla?" Her tone became defensive but curious.

"I don't know how to tell you this... but I'm her son."

Carrie squinted. She stared into his eyes, let out a light chuckle, before her lips formed into a frown. "My sister has been dead for sixteen years and she never had any children."

"She had one. By Silas Kinnard. Born on November 22, 1997. She died during childbirth, giving birth to me."

Her eyes grew wide. "It can't be." She got closer, placing her hands on the sides of his face, running her fingers along his cheekbones. "The letter told me that the baby didn't make it. How do I know you're telling me the truth?"

That's when he noticed the birthmark on her arm. He took her arm, placing his thumb on her mark. "This is how..." He lifted his sleeve, showing her his birthmark.

Her hand clasped over her mouth. She began mumbling, tears forming in her eyes. "My god, this is real."

Jackson smiled, "Hi Aunt Carrie."

She wrapped her hands around his shoulders, hugging him tightly. They stood in the doorway, in silence, neither of them had the words to describe this remarkable moment.

***

She took him inside, getting him settled in the kitchen while asking a dozen questions about his journey.

"You must be exhausted," She said, pouring them glasses of lemonade from her fridge. "You drove all the way here from Chicago?"

"Yes. I spent a lot of time trying to find you." He said, taking a sip from his cup. "Well, before I knew exactly who I was looking for. Any family really."

"All this time, you were alive." She shook her head in disbelief. "I can't believe they kept you from us."

"It was a secret adoption. But my adoptive parents are dead." He told her. The less she knew about Hank and the others, the better. "Speaking of parents, what did you know about my father?"

"Oh Silas," She rested her fist on her chin. "He was a strange man. Around the time he and your mother met, she began to act strangely too. Sneaking out late and coming back at dawn. Whatever it was, I know he had something to do with it."

Beads of sweat formed around his hairline. He figured she hadn't known about them being shifters. Which meant she couldn't know about him.

"Sounds like you didn't like him very much," Jackson suggested.

"I didn't have any issues with him personally. I just wanted my sister back. I miss her so much." Carrie's lowered her eyes. She reached over and grabbed his hand. Carrie's eyes lifted and she smiled. "So, are you in school?"

"No ma'am. I was homeschooled until I turned sixteen."

"Beautiful and smart, just like your mother. It's a shame you never got to know her. But I'm so thankful that I get to know you, now. And I want you to stay. As long as you'd like. I run a small bakery in town, you can come by and help me out. I could use an extra hand."

"I'd love that." He replied, holding her hand tighter.

And it was at that moment, Jackson felt something he had never felt in the sixteen years he lived with Hank. Love radiated from this moment that filled his heart with the sense of belonging he had been searching for his entire life.

***

Carrie took Jackson to the market with her to pick up some things for dinner. She wanted to show him around town and introduce him to some of the locals. The people in Marksville were nothing like the ones he encountered back in Chicago. Not that he spent much time around humans. Shifters mostly kept themselves separated from humans and only interacted if it was necessary. He was homeschooled, they mostly ate what they hunted, and he planned to live at his father's cabin whenever he went back home. But he wasn't planning on it anytime soon. According to Hank, Jackson's father left behind a trust fund for him. One of the few nice things Hank did regarding Jackson's family was protect and allow him access to the account his father left for him.

"Oh, Jackson! There's someone else I want you to meet!" Carrie said, pulling him in the direction of isle 4 as he cradled a handful of items in his arms.

Suddenly, heat coursed through his veins, and his senses heightened. The scent hit him like a semi coming at full speed. A shifter. Someone was nearby. But his ability to sense them was stronger than he had ever felt before.

"Jackson, meet Delilah Hope Simmons. She's about your age. I used to babysit her when she was a wee little thing." Carrie said scrunching her face in a smile.

The cashier, with her smooth dark brown complexion and thick hair tied back in two curly ponytails, was already looking at Jackson before his eyes met hers. It was as if time slowed down, and Carrie's voice became a distant hum.

"Hi." She greeted him softly. Slowly scanning the items Carrie placed on her belt.

"Hi." He responded. Their eyes still locked on one another.

"Delilah, Jackson is my nephew. From Chicago." Carrie told her.

"I didn't know you had a nephew, Ms. Lakota," Delilah said, snapping out of her daze and attending to the rest of the items.

"Yes. My late sister Carla. This is her son. He was adopted."

Jackson gave a slight wave, wearing a pressed lip smile.

"Wow. That's cool." Delilah replied, glancing at Carrie before focusing back on Jackson. "It's nice to meet you, Jackson."

"You too." He said.

"I wish we could stay and chat, but I've got a lot to do this evening. Nice seeing you as always Delilah!" Carrie said, rushing to grab her bagged items, handing them to Jackson.

"Bye Ms. Lakota." Said Delilah, giving a polite smile before moving on to the next customer in line.

Carrie led Jackson back to the car, he looked behind his shoulder, but Delilah was out of his sight. The strong sensation he had in the store was now gone. Whoever this girl was, made the beast inside him long for more of her. And he knew she felt it too.

CHAPTER 3

Icy cold water rushed against her skin as she struggled to keep her head above water. Taking short breaths, Delilah became submerged, being pulled down into the depths by an unknown force. She flailed her arms around, trying to push herself back up to the surface. The water around her turned a bloody red as she tried to scream while holding in the last bit of air she had left. That's when she saw a figure standing above the water. They reached their hand inside, clasping onto hers. They pulled her up towards the surface, and she could hear their faint voice as she got closer.

"Don't worry, I've got you." They said.

They pulled her from the water, and she took a deep breath, letting it all out as she gasped for air. Kneeling in front of her was Jackson. Neither of them said a word, they just stared at each other. And he smiled. Seconds later, the unknown force pulled her back underwater. This time, taking Jackson along. As they sank deeper into the dark waters, Jackson didn't let go of her hand. Her chest tightened as she slowly lost consciousness. And still, he didn't let go.

Delilah awoke from her dream, drenched in sweat and choking up water that wasn't there. Heaving and clutching her chest. She tried to calm herself down, reassuring herself that it was only a nightmare. Her third one this week. But this one was different. She wasn't alone. She rubbed her eyes, taking off her nightshirt and turning her pillow over before laying back down.

Jackson… who are you?

***

The next morning, Jackson awoke to Carrie making breakfast downstairs. As he made his way into the kitchen, there was a knock at the door.

"Could you answer that, sweetheart?" Carrie asked.

"Sure." He walked toward the door, and hitting him like a wave, was that feeling again. From the market. He opened it, and there standing, was Delilah.

She stood holding a bag of garden tools, looking up at him with bold, brown eyes. Purple glitter eyeshadow sparkled on her eyelids.

"Hello, Jackson." Delilah greeted. "I'm here to return these to Ms. Lakota."

"Um, yeah, sure come in." He moved to the side, giving her room to come through. "Aunt Carrie, we have a visitor."

"Who is it?" Carrie walked out from the kitchen, "Oh, good morning Delilah! What brings you by?" She asked excitedly.

"I just came to return your gardening tools." Said Delilah holding out the bag. "My momma's done using them."

"Why thank you, dear! I nearly forgot about them." Carrie took the bag from Delilah, placing it on a nearby table. "Oh that reminds me, Jackson, maybe Delilah can be of some company while you're in town. I know you don't want to spend all your time with boring ol' me."

"That sounds nice, actually," Jackson said, smiling at Delilah. "What is there to do around here?" He asked her.

Delilah shrugged, "Depends on what you're into. Lots of people hang out at the lake. There's a bar that hosts karaoke in the afternoons."

"I'm kind of a night guy." He replied.

Delilah's lips formed into a small grin. "Me too." Her grin then turned into a slight frown, her eyebrows raised. "Uh… I mean, I'm a night person too! Not like an actual guy! That's not what I meant." Delilah giggled, slapping her forehead.

Jackson laughed. "I know what you meant. It's cool."

Delilah scratched the back of her neck, "Anyway…. I gotta go. Jackson, I'll um… see you around?"

"Yeah, sure."

"Bye Ms. Lakota!" Delilah turns, opening the door and scurrying out before Carrie could say bye.

"Such a sweetheart, isn't she Jackson?" Carrie said, heading back into the kitchen.

Jackson walked towards the door, peeking his head out. He squinted, confused when he didn't see Delilah. She had literally just left out moments ago and was now nowhere to be seen. Tonight was a full moon, and he knew she would show up again. Even though purebred shifters like himself could turn whenever they wanted to, it was an unwritten rule among the community that they try to blend as much as possible. Which meant remaining in human form while in the presence of non-shifters, and turning mostly during the full moon, the only time feys could turn. There was something peculiar about this girl, and Jackson was determined to find out what it was.

***

Jackson crept downstairs as Carrie slept, slowly opening the door and closing it behind him without making a sound. The one thing Jackson liked about the countryside, was that the woods were everywhere. It was the perfect place to turn without the risk of being spotted. There were woods about half a mile from Carrie's house, where Jackson went as the sunset and the sky turned a deep, indigo blue. When he reached the woods, it was quiet. Nothing but the sounds of bugs buzzing in the distance.

The thing about pure-borns is they had control over how, and when they turned. He could shift into the beast instantly, without removing his clothes like feys had to do. When they were newly turned anyway. As their bodies adjusted, the process became easier.

He relaxed his shoulders, as he began to take the shape of the beast, molding itself into its natural form. His bones snapping and stretching as his skin transformed into the rough exterior of an animal. He howled as his vision heightened, running through the trees, the night air whistling across his fur. Being in his true form was nothing like being in his human form. None of the problems of the world mattered when he turned. He could just, be.

He could hear the pressing of leaves coming from behind him. Getting in defense mode, he turned around swiftly, letting out a low growl. Standing ahead of him, was another shifter. His defense immediately dropped as he drew closer. The beast peered into his eyes. It was Delilah. He recognized her unmistakable scent.

She was so beautiful. Her absinthe green eyes matching his. It was the one common trait that all shifters had when they turned. With Jackson standing just inches away, she took off running. He chased after her until she came to a stop. Turning to face him, she pounced. They fell to the ground, Delilah hovering over him. She licked his face, rubbing her snout gently against his fur. He let her, allowing her dominance to take over while he licked her face back.

A growl emerged from behind them followed by barking. Delilah and Jackson got up, and Jackson was once again in defense mode. Another shifter, with his eyes set on Jackson, immediately charged at him as the two began to tussle. Delilah began to bark, trying to break them apart. Suddenly another shifter approached, and the one who attacked Jackson backed away, leaving him alone. Jackson and Delilah stood side by side as the other two stood across from them. The one who attacked Jackson let out a whimper as the other one barked at him and growled. They both turned and ran off.

Jackson turned to Delilah, who was sitting on the ground, now in her human form. He immediately turned back, and they both just sat there waiting for the other to speak. Delilah's mouth moved like she was fixing to say something. But she got up, twirling the necklace around her neck, and darted off between the trees.

"Wait! Come back!" Jackson called out to her, running to catch up. But just like the last time, she was gone.

CHAPTER 4

The next evening, Jackson went to the market to catch Delilah as she ended her shift. He waited outside, until closing. As the last customer left, another employee followed, waving at Delilah as she locked the doors behind them. When the cars left the parking lot, Jackson went up to the door, knocking as Delilah turned off the lights. With her purse over her arm, her forehead creased. She unlocked the door, letting him inside. She lowered her head, as she clenched the straps of her purse.

"Hello, Jackson." She uttered.

"Hey, I was just coming by because I wanted to talk." He said, with his hands in his pockets. "If you have time."

"Sure. I'm assuming it's about last night."

"What was that all about? And why did you run from me?"

"I was just playing with you. I got a little excited, I don't usually share that kind of connection with other shifters I've met."

"So you feel it too?"

"Yeah. But I'm sure you knew that already." She said with a smile." Sorry I ran off. I got nervous. I'm a bit of a spaz. I don't do well in awkward situations if you've noticed." She chuckled faintly.

"What about the others? The ones that attacked me last night?"

"Oh, that's just Stephan and Bryce." She said, rolling her eyes. "The one that attacked you is Stephan. My ex-boyfriend."

"Ah, ex-boyfriend. Awesome."

"Don't worry about them. They're just some local idiots with nothing else better to do." Delilah glanced behind Jackson, as a small group got out of a car and headed towards the market. She sneered as they approached. "Speaking of local idiots…"

Jackson turned around, as Bryce and Stephan pushed their way through the door.

"Delilah Hope Simmons!" Bryce called out, looking around at the empty store. "Oh, my apologies. Are yall closed?" He held his hand over his chest, laughing.

"Why are you here Bryce?" Delilah huffed as Stephan stood over her.

"I just wanted to stop by and formally introduce myself to the new guy in town." Bryce stood in front of Jackson, his hands behind his back. "We seem to have crossed paths last night if you recall?"

"I recall your friend attacking me," Jackson said, wearing a blank expression, his jaw clenched.

"I attacked you because you were all up on my girl," Stephan said, brushing shoulders with Jackson. The sharp tension between the four of them could cut through steel.

"Delilah came after me. Sounds like your problem, not mine." Jackson said.

"I'm not your girl anymore! I've said it a million times!" Delilah yelled at Stephan. "Now get on before I call the cops!"

"Now, now, there's no need for that," Bryce said, holding up his hand. "Stephan leave him alone. Stop acting like an animal and go wait outside. Now!" He ordered.

Stephan backed away, through the door. He kicked over a pile of shopping baskets as he slammed the door behind him.

"As I was saying, my name is Bryce Barbeau. I'm kind of a big deal in this town. And you are?" He held out his hand, signaling for a handshake.

"None of your business." He replied. Jackson looked down at his extended hand, then back up at Bryce. His expression remained hard and disinterested.

Bryce winced at him. "Well, have it your way then. I'll be seeing you around."

He turned to leave the store, meeting the others in his car. Stephan grabbed a blade from his pocket, walked over to Delilah's car, kneeling, and slashing a hole in one of her tires. The boys laughed, getting in Bryce's car and driving away.

"Dammit!" Delilah ran out to her car, kneeling to look at the gash. "I hate him!" She groaned.

Jackson stood next to her. "I can give you a ride home." He offered. "You live near my aunt right?"

She looked up at him, relieved. "Thanks. I really appreciate it." She said as they went over to his station wagon, "Hey, you know you don't have to worry about those guys."

He got in on the driver's side. "I'm not worried. I've come across much more intimidating guys in Chicago. And they don't scare me either." He said.

"Good. Bryce is all talk anyway. And Stephan is a little slow in the head, but he won't go too far."

Jackson looked over at her as they drove away. "And that guy was your boyfriend?"

"We dated for like three weeks. Don't judge me." She laughed.

"No judgment here. Okay, maybe a little." He joked.

Delilah playfully nudged his shoulder. "I'm serious. He's a part of my past that I would like to forget."

"So, what's your deal anyway?" Jackson asked, changing the tone of their conversation.

She toyed with a lock of her hair. "Well, I'm pure born but half-bred technically. I'm only a shifter on my dad's side. He left when I was ten. I ain't seen him since."

"So your mother isn't a fey?" He asked.

"Nope. She's a witch. And so am I."

Jackson's eyes bulged. "You're what?"

"Half witch, half shifter. It's actually a common mix here in Louisiana. That guy you met, Bryce, he's half-witch too. Well, warlock. That's what we call male practitioners of witchcraft."

"I know what a warlock is. I just didn't think they still existed." He said.

She narrowed her eyes. "Of course you didn't think so. The council has tried its best to hide any traces of us for centuries. We aren't as strong as we once were. But, we're around."

"Wow. So, wait… is that how you've been able to disappear so fast?" Jackson asked.

"Disappear? No way. I'm not that good of a witch yet." She giggled, pulling a necklace from under her shirt. "I used this. It's a time stopper. I simply just pause the clock whenever I want to get out of a bad or awkward situation. Then press it again when I'm done." She grinned.

"That… sounds extremely dangerous."

"It can be. That's why I only use it for small stuff." She stuffed it back in her shirt. "Maybe we can stop time and do something fun together? I have a bunch of cool stuff I can show you. If you'd like it."

His face flushed. "I don't know. Maybe."

"So, what about you?" She asked. "You just show up here out of nowhere on Ms. Lakota's doorstep. What's your deal?"

Jackson thought about Hank and Kayla. "I'm purebred. Fey mother, pure-born father. But I was adopted. It's complicated."

"What is life if it ain't complicated, right?" Delilah sighed.

"I guess you're right."

They shared a quick glance before Delilah noticed them coming to the turn that led to her house. "My house is over there." She pointed.

He pulled up to her house, turning the engine off. He got out to walk her to her door.

"Thanks for the ride, Jackson. I would invite you in but my mother's a buzzkill. She never lets me bring friends over. But maybe we can hang out sometime this week. When I'm not at school or working." Delilah suggested.

"Sounds good. I don't have a cell phone though." He told her.

She cringed. "What are you, stuck in the 90s?"

They both laughed.

"It's fine. I know Ms. Lakota's landline number. And you know where I live. See you later, alligator." She smiled, before unlocking the door and going inside.

A smile slipped through his lips as he headed back to his car.

Wow, a witch.

Chapter 5

Jackson spent most of his first week at Carrie's bakery, and when they weren't bonding over French breads and cakes, he was learning more about his mother, and family history. There was so much time missed that he could never get back, but what was missed didn't matter now. All that mattered now, was the time he had left.

Jackson wiped down the windows at the store while Carrie sat at one of the tables reading through papers. She drew in a long breath, raking her fingers through her hair. He stopped wiping, looking over at her, concerned.

"Auntie, are you alright?" He asked, walking over to her.

"I wish I could say I was." She replied.

He took a seat next to her, "What is it?" He looked at the papers she held in her hand.

"The city wants to take my home. They sent me a letter saying I had three weeks to move."

"What? That can't be right!" He took the letter from her, skimming through it. "It says something about bulldozing the area to build a casino. How can they do this? This has to be illegal!"

"Unfortunately, they can. Our grandfather sold the Choctaw land in the 80s. It was bought by the Barbeau estate and the family has been paying property taxes ever since."

Barbeau. A trace of bitterness filled his mouth as he thought about his encounter with Bryce. Jackson knew this couldn't have been a coincidence. For whatever reason, this guy was making things personal. Between his unexplainable connection with Delilah and the boys in this town being assholes, Jackson was starting to think he made the wrong choice by coming here. Too much was going on already and he hadn't even been in Marksville that long.

He placed his arm around her. "Don't worry Aunt Carrie, we'll figure something out."

In an instant, his nostrils flared, and he could smell the scent of another shifter nearby. One that wasn't Delilah. He looked over his shoulder, and that's when he saw Bryce, standing outside leering at them through the glass with his hands in his pockets. Jackson's temples throbbed with rage.

"Hey auntie, I'm gonna take out the trash. I'll be right back."

She nodded as he got up, collecting the garbage from the storage bins and heading to the back. As soon as he opened the back doors, Bryce was waiting.

"Good to see you again Jackson." He said with a smirk.

Jackson dropped the bags, gripping Bryce by the collar of his shirt and pushing him against the brick wall. "I don't know what your problem is with me, but you leave my aunt out of it." Jackson threatened, gritting his teeth.

"Whoa, relax now," Bryce said with his hands up. "This is a $200 shirt. And if you really want to help your aunt, I suggest you let me go."

Jackson let go. "What do you want?"

rolling his shoulders, Bryce adjusted his collar. "What I want, is simple. *Akwụkwọ nke chi.*"

"What are you talking about?"

"The Book of Gods. It's a spellbook" Bryce said.

"What does that have to do with me?"

"It has a lot to do with you Jackson because it's your ticket to true freedom. Meet me back out here in an hour. We'll go for a little ride." Bryce walked off, and Jackson tossed the garbage bags in a nearby dumpster before going back inside.

Jackson wondered what Bryce meant by true freedom, and what kind of scheme he had up his sleeve.

***

An hour later, Jackson did as Bryce asked. He met him outside after closing the shop to settle whatever this nonsense was about a spellbook. Bryce waited in his silver Camaro, as Jackson walked over to the passenger side, reluctant as he calmed himself before getting in. Bryce wasted no time speeding out of the parking lot.

"Start talking," Jackson demanded.

"Listen, I know you think I'm an asshole. But I'm not your enemy." Bryce said. "I believe that we are all brothers. Us shifters. We should roam this earth as we were meant to be. No rules from the higher-ups telling us how we should live our lives. Who we can mate with. When we can turn. Don't you agree?"

Jackson shrugged. He thought about his upbringing and didn't disagree with the idea of the council not breathing down their necks with strict codes, but Bryce didn't need to know that.

"What are you saying?" Jackson asked.

"What I'm saying is, we don't have to live that way anymore. This world can be ours. But in order for us to make that happen, I need that spellbook. That's where you come in. There's only one copy of that book that exists. And Delilah has it."

Jacksons felt an ache in the pit of his stomach at the mention of Delilah's name. "So why do you need me?"

"Because you're going to get that book from her."

"I'm not stealing anything from Delilah!"

"Then I guess your aunt doesn't want to keep her house."

"There must be another way. Why can't you just ask her for it? Or steal it yourself?"

Bryce laughed. "Do you really think she'd give it to me? If it were that easy we wouldn't be having this conversation. The book is protected by the house. It's been passed down her family for generations. The only way that anyone who isn't a direct descendant can access the book is by being invited in." He continued.

"This sounds ridiculous." Jackson shook his head.

"Well, it's the truth. That mother of hers is strict and far from stupid. She never allows Delilah to have company over. That idiot Stephan dated her for three weeks and he couldn't even charm her enough to get past the damn porch." Bryce said.

"And what makes you think I'll be any different?"

"I've seen how she looks at you. How you two were in the woods that night. I don't know what it is, and quite frankly I don't give a damn. All I want is that book. You have a choice, Jackson. I reckon you're smart enough to make the right one."

They rode to a vacant lot a few miles away from the shopping district where Carrie's bakery was. Bryce stopped the car, pointing ahead.

"Right over that hill is a bunker. It's where I and my crew hang out. Bring the book here." Bryce told him.

"How do I know what I'm looking for?" Jackson asked.

"It's a small red book with leather binding. There's a symbol on the front. Like an eye. You'll know it when you see it." Bryce turned off the engine. "Why don't you come down and have a drink or two? I'll introduce you to the fellas."

"Nah, I don't think so," Jackson replied.

"Suit yourself then. You have a week to get me that book. I'll be in touch."

With the snap of a finger, Jackson went from the front seat of Bryce's car to the couch in his aunt's living room.

"What the hell?" He blinked rapidly, gripping the couch cushions.

The jingling of keys from outside caught his attention as the front door opened.

"My goodness!" Carrie exclaimed, "How did you get here so fast? And I thought you had plans?"

"They changed." He said, still mentally recovering.

"Ah well, there's always tomorrow." Carrie grinned, heading upstairs.

The phone rang, Jackson leaned over the coffee table, glancing at the caller ID. It was Delilah. He picked it up swiftly, "Hey!" She couldn't have called at a worse time.

"What are you up to?" She asked. "I'm free tonight."

"I've gotta help my aunt with some things. Sorry, I'd love to see you though. It's just not a good time tonight."

"Oh, well how's tomorrow?" She asked.

"Tomorrow's perfect."

"Sounds good. I'll come by then." She said with excitement. "So, what were you up to today? I hope Louisiana is treating you good." She said.

His stomach heaved at the thought of Bryce. "It's alright so far I guess. I'm sure it'll be better when I see you."

Delilah's face went warm. "Yeah, well I'll try my best to be a good tour guide." She laughed slightly.

"Can't wait." He said softly.

"Same." Delilah said with a smile.

"Well, I'm gonna get some rest. How about instead of you coming by tomorrow, I just pick you up from work?" He asked.

"I'd like that. See you then?"

"Sounds like a plan. See you then."

They ended their call. Jackson sighed heavily, running his hands across his face. He just wanted this nightmare of a day to be over. He had no idea how he was going to get this book for Bryce. But he blocked out those negative thoughts and focused on the good side. He would be spending time with Delilah again.

Chapter 6

The next day, Jackson picked Delilah up after her morning shift at work. She ditched her work uniform and sported a pair of dark blue denim shorts and a black button-up top with yellow sunflowers. She got in on the passenger side, pointing at Jackson's OutKast t-shirt.

"You've got good taste. You should let me borrow that some time." She said, pulling her hair out of the white tie that held her bouncy coils in place.

"I could take it off right now and you can have it." He said in a facetious tone. "It would probably look better on you anyway."

Delilah giggled, giving a dismissive wave of her hand.

"So where to? He asked.

"You up for a turn?"

"Turn?" Jackson asked.

"Yeah, I know a spot."

"In the daytime? I don't know if that's a good idea."

"It is with this…" She pulled out her necklace, inclining her head.

"Let's go then." He agreed.

Delilah gave him directions to Tunica lake, a hotspot for Marksville locals. They arrived, pulling into a small parking lot, where two other cars are parked. One was a minivan, which gave Jackson the impression that a family might be around.

"There are other people here?" Jackson asked, becoming skeptical of her plan.

"Yeah, but they won't know a thing." She assured him, pulling the time stopper from under her blouse and holding his hand. "It'll be fine."

Jackson watched as she used her thumb to press the center of the clock. The little second hand stopped, she moved the hour and minute handles backward. He looked around to see if he could spot any differences. But nothing looked or felt strange.

"So that's it?" He asked.

"Yep. We've got about two hours. After that, well, I don't wanna stick around to find out. Come on! The lake is just through here!" Delilah said as she shifted into the beast and took off running in the direction of the woods.

Jackson ran not too far behind her, shifting and trying to keep up with Delilah. It wasn't until he began picking up speed when he noticed the wind felt stiff. Gazing up at the trees, there were no ripples along the leaves. No swaying of the branches. He came to an opening behind the trees that gave way to Olympic blue waters. To his left, there was a family sitting at the edge of the water. A father and two children. There was another man in a boat out on the lake, fishing. All frozen in place. Delilah walked into the lake, splashing her paws against the water, paddling around. The stillness of the water was mesmerizing. The ripples following Delilah as she moved along the water, as if she was a part of it. Everything about her was so graceful and soft. No matter which form he saw her in. Human or shifted. Jackson went in, frisking his hind legs as they swam around each other, antagonizing the other playfully.

An hour went by and Delilah grew tired, going underneath the water, Jackson switched back to his human form, looking around the surface for her to reappear.

"Delilah?" He called out.

Suddenly she sprung up behind him back in human form, locking her arms around his shoulders.

"Did I scare you?" She asked, giggling.

"A little," He said, holding on to her forearms trying to keep them both afloat.

They swam around like that for a little while longer, enjoying the freedom of a world that temporarily didn't exist, just for them. They went back to the shore, collapsing into nearby grass where the sun beamed down on them. Jackson turned his head, watching the sun rays absorb into Delilah's dark sienna tone skin. He turned his head as she looked at him, his wet shirt melting onto his toned arms.

"I've never been turned that long during the day before." He said.

"Amazing, huh?" She grinned with her eyes closed, facing back at the sun.

"Yeah." He replied.

Delilah turned to her side, resting her elbow in the grass. "Sometimes, I wish I could stay like that forever." She said. "Do you ever feel like that?"

"Nah. I like being human. When it's worth it."

"How do you mean?" She asked.

"When I get to experience things like this." He said. "That's why I left Chicago to find my family. I want to feel what it's really like to live. I love who I am, I just want both parts of me to feel equal."

"So what are your plans now that you're here?"

"I want to spend as much time as I can with Aunt Carrie. After that, I plan on traveling for a while. Just seeing what the country has to offer. Then I'll settle down back up north."

Delilah's eyes grew big. "Lucky! My momma acts like she never wants me to leave this place. But if I ever do travel, I wanna be a nurse like my momma, or something like that. But instead of humans, I'll help other shifters. Like feys when they first get turned and have no one to show them the ropes."

"Sounds like a great plan. When I leave, you can tag along. If you want." He said. "I think we'd have a blast together."

"I'd love to." Her eyes lit up at the idea of exploring the country with him, and finally getting out of Louisiana. She pulled the necklace from beneath her half-dry blouse, restarting the clock and adjusting the time.

"You wanna go back to my house? My momma's working a double shift at the hospital." She suggested.

"Sure."

He had been having so much fun with her, that he forgot about Bryce. This was the invitation he needed. Worry gnawed at him, unsure of how he would ever pull this off. But he had to get it done. Carrie's livelihood depended on it.

***

Back at Delilah's house, she led Jackson to her room, tossing her purse on the floor and plopping down on her bed. He looked around at the random hangings of movie posters on her walls. Mostly 90s cult classic horror movies and a few musicals like

West Side Story. It was an odd mix, but that was the kind of girl Delilah was. Odd and distinctive, but he loved that about her.

He thought about his relationship with Kayla. It was never like this. They never bonded over music or even talked about their futures as shifters. His attachment to her was more so due to familiarity. There was no doubt that they cared about each other, but Jackson knew his relationship with Kayla would never be more than late afternoon hook-up's when her father wasn't home. Hank and his kids had no sense of adventure or curiosity. Not like him. Not like Delilah.

She pulled up a music app on her phone, connecting it to the Bluetooth speakers. She tossed the phone to Jackson.

"Pick something." She said.

He caught the phone, scrolling her playlist. "OutKast. Gasoline Dreams." He handed her back the phone as the music played.

Delilah gasped. "One of my top 10 tracks of all time! And perfect for setting the mood!" She smiled. "I hope you didn't waste all of your energy on our little trip. The real fun is just beginning. Come, sit next to me." She gestures with her palm.

She smirked as he came over to sit. She rolled over to open her bedside dresser drawer. She then pulled out a small bottle containing a dark blue liquid.

Jackson's eyes glinted with curiosity. "Do I even want to know what that is?" He asked.

"Have you ever wanted to talk to the dead?" She asked, her eyes focused on the bottle. "I mean like, your parents. People close to you. Like you would with a Ouija board."

His eyes bulged. "That's a weird question. He said through a light chuckle. "I've never thought about it."

"Do you want to?" Her eyes moved to meet his. "It's safe. I promise. It's just a potion I learned to make in middle school. I used it to contact my grandma. But I've only taken it a few times, and I've never shared it with anyone else."

She handed him the bottle, he twirled it between his fingers. The thought of his parents crossed his mind.

"What will it do to me?" He asked.

"It'll just feel like you're dreaming. And you can leave anytime you want. You're in control."

He took in a deep breath, "Okay." He agreed, twisting open the top.

Delilah grinned. "Just take two drops, lay back, relax, and let me lead the way."

He did as instructed, tilting his head back and taking two drops. He handed her the bottle, and she took two as well. She screwed the top back on, putting it back on her dresser. They both laid back, Delilah gripped his hand. Jackson's heartbeat began to increase, his chest tightening with unease as they both stared at the ceiling. The sounds of OutKast becoming slow, and faint as his pupils dilated. Then... there was darkness.

Chapter 7

In the blink of an eye, Jackson was transported to an empty, dark room. He was sitting cross-legged, with the glare of a candle in front of him. He looked around, sweat trickled down his spine. Sitting across from him, was Delilah.

"Don't be afraid, just relax, and keep an open mind." She said.

"What do I do now?" He asked.

"Repeat after me… Mother of spirits, send to me the ones I wish to speak…"

He followed. "Mother of spirits, send to me the ones I wish to speak."

The flame in the candle went out, and he could no longer see Delilah. Suddenly, he could hear footsteps coming from behind. A chill went through him, as a pair of cold hands touched his forearms. Soft skin brushed against his cheek, long, silky hair draped over his shoulder.

"My son, I am here…" A soft voice uttered into his ear.

He twirled around, his face turned a crimson red as the candlelight returned, burning brighter this time. Sitting before him, was his mother.

"Mom…" His lips trembled.

She cupped the sides of his face with her palms, her lips turning upwards into a gentle smile. "You have your father's eyes." She said.

Jackson couldn't believe what he was seeing. He ran his hands across her face. She felt so real. She was real, to him. "Mom, I… I don't know what to say. I can't believe it's really you."

The flame grew brighter. His mother's smile went away. "Jackson, I cannot stay. But I need to tell you something before I go."

"No, you can't leave." He begged, tightly gripping her hands.

"You have to save her Jackson. It's the only way." His mother said. "I love you, son."

The flame overpowered them both, and she was gone. A wave of nausea hit as Jackson's brain flicked like a light switch and he was back in Delilah's bed. He screamed as Delilah shook his shoulders, calling his name to calm him down.

"Jackson, it's me," she said. "She placed her hands on his head. "Relax. It's over."

He looked into her eyes, as she stroked the hair damp with sweat that curled over his ear. He finally caught his breath, fresh energy filling him as his anxiety settled. He placed his hand over hers, the warmth from her skin made him feel safe. A half-smile emerged from her lips, as her face, slowly drew closer to his.

Suddenly, the door opened. Delilah turned her face away from his, jolting upright.

"What on earth is this?" Delilah's mother stood in the doorway, her hand resting on her hip with one eyebrow raised.

"Momma, this is Jackson. Ms. Lakota's nephew."

Jackson stood up, "Nice to meet you, Mrs. Simmons." He greeted with his arms at his sides.

Her mother's eyes squinted. "Mrs. Lakota's nephew?"

"Yeah. Didn't you know his mom back in the day? Carla?" Delilah asked.

Her mother's eyebrows raised, "Carla is your mother?" She asked.

"Yeah. Were you two friends?" Jackson asked.

"Something like that, yes." She crossed her arms, her eyes studying Jackson's features. "You can call me Ms. Mary by the way." She said. "I thought Carla's baby died during childbirth?" She asked.

"Thought. obviously." Delilah huffed.

Mary faked a smile, "Well, god bless. What a miracle." She was looking at him but her eyes were somber. Her mind seemed to be in another place. She cast a veiled glance at her daughter, then back at Jackson. "Well then, it was lovely meeting you young man. But Delilah has chores so you should be going."

"No, I don't." Delilah cut in.

Mary shot her daughter a look. "Don't back-talk me, missy."

"Guess I'll head out then. Bye Delilah." Jackson waved before sliding past Mary and heading out.

"Bye!" Delilah called out to him.

Mary closed Delilah's door behind him, her mouth set in a hard line as a look of anger shot from her eyes.

Delilah's eyes went round as she slouched. "I know, no company in the house without your permission."

Mary slammed her hand down against the dresser that sat by Delilah's door. "I want you to stay away from him. Do you understand me?"

Delilah frowned, "What's your problem? We're just friends."

"I don't care! I said stay away from him and I mean it!" Mary shouted.

"Why?... Oh wait, it's because he's a shifter, right?" Delilah groaned. "This is why dad left. You hate shifters and you took it out on him. Now you take it out on me!"

Mary's mouth dropped. "Frank was a liar and a cheater. That's why he left. And you better watch your mouth young lady!"

Delilah's every muscle tensed as the room began to shake. Pictures fell from the walls, her ceiling fan became detached, dangling by its wires before falling. Mary dodged to the side to avoid being hit. She drew back against the dresser.

Realizing what she had done, Delilah relaxed. Her eyes tearing up. "Momma, I'm sorry. I didn't mean to do that. But I'm not staying away from Jackson. I can't. Me and him were connected, momma."

"Delilah… You're seventeen. You don't understand what you feel."

Delilah ran past her mother, down the hall, and into the bathroom, slamming the door. Mary went after her, pulling at the knob of the bathroom door.

"Delilah! Open this door!" She yelled.

"No!" Delilah screamed from the other side.

Mary rubbed her throbbing temples, taking in a long breath with her back against the door. She knew there was only one way she could get through to Delilah, even though it was the last thing on earth she wanted to do. She went to her bedroom, walking over to the closet, and turning on the little switch light. She reached on the top shelf, pulling out a book. She flipped to the back of the book, pulling out a small photo, clutching it against her chest. She went back to the bathroom, kneeling and sliding the photo under the door.

"This is for you," Mary said.

Delilah, sitting with her back to the tub, holding her knees to her chest crawled over to grab the photo. It was a picture of a man holding a newborn baby.

"What is this?" She asked her mother.

"When I was young, I was in love with a man. We were supposed to get married, but things changed." Despair rose in Mary's voice as she reminisced. "He left me for another woman, a month after you were born. His name was Silas.

"What are you saying, momma?"

"I'm saying, that this man in the photo was your real father. Silas Kinnard. When he left me, I didn't know how I'd raise a shifter on my own. Not long after that, I met Frank."

Delilah shook her head in disbelief. "No, this can't be right."

"Delilah…" Mary's voice shook, "Silas is Jackson's father.

Delilah froze, crumpling the photo between her fist. Shame washed over her, as she forced down a sick feeling. Her whole world suddenly came crashing down around her. Jackson was her brother. Her mind became a scrambled mess as she attempted to piece this all together. Mary used a spell to open the door, standing in the doorway, sorrow shredding her insides.

"I know this is hard for you, and I regret keeping this secret for so long. I'm so sorry." Mary inched closer to her.

"All this time, my life was a lie," Delilah said under her breath. Too heartbroken to look her mother in the eyes.

"I didn't mean for it to turn out this way. I promise. I never thought in a million years that it would come to this. All these years, nobody knew he was alive." Mary kneeled next to her daughter, placing her hand on her shoulder.

Delilah jerked away. "This isn't about Jackson! What does him being alive have to do with you lying to me about my father? The only reason you're even telling me this now is because you caught us together!"

"Can you blame me? If I hadn't come in when I did…"

Delilah covered her ears, blocking out the thought. "Momma just stop it! This is all your fault! I don't want to hear anymore!"

She got up, running out of the bathroom and out of the house. The house shook as her mother called out for her, but Delilah was gone. Shifting into the beast and leaving a trail of wrath from her fury that burned within.

CHAPTER 8

Jackson got back to the house, slouching with his head hung. He couldn't get his mother's face, her touch out of his mind. It was like nothing he had ever experienced before. He trudged up to his room, falling onto his bed. His mother's words replayed in his head.

You have to save her, it's the only way…

He wondered what his mother meant by save her. Maybe she meant to save Carrie or even Delilah? He thought about Delilah and how he would explain the missing book to her when the time came. It seemed that no matter what he chose, it would result in hurting someone he cared about.

There was a knock on his bedroom door. He sat up, "Come in." He said.

Carrie opened the door, peeking in. "May I come in?" She asked?

"Of course. What is it?"

Carrie slid through the door, Walking over to his bed. "I heard you come in, and I just wanted to check on you. Call it intuition but I just got a feeling, so I'm just making sure you were alright."

He gazed down, away from her face as he forced a closed-lip smile. "Actually, I'm a bit shaken up." He said, trying to find a way to explain to her what he saw. "I saw my mom. She came to me in a dream."

"Oh dear," Carrie pressed her fingers over her mouth. She took him in her arms, hugging him closely. "You know, it's perfectly normal for dead relatives to visit us in our dreams. It means her spirit is watching over you."

"I hope so."

"Did she say anything?"

Jackson shook his head, "No."

"Well, I'm sure she'll find a way to speak to you. Dreams like that don't always make sense. But they will."

They pulled away from each other, Carrie cupped his chin with her palm.

"I really am glad you're here." She said. "When all is said and done, family is everything. And no matter what, we'll always have each other." She said. "Now you get some rest. And if Carla visits you again, tell her I said she still owes me twenty bucks." She chuckled, as she got up to leave the room.

The corners of his mouth raised, "Love you, Aunt Carrie."

"Love you too dear." She said as the door closed behind her.

Jackson thought about what she said. Family meant everything to him, and he wasn't about to let anyone hurt, or take anything away from his.

***

The following day, he had his plan set in motion to get the book from Delilah's house. The hard part was over, getting her to invite him in. Now he just needed a time when neither Delilah nor her mother Mary would be home. He tried to spot anything resembling a red book while in her house the day before but saw nothing. It was Monday and Delilah had school. She normally went to work afterward. Her mother left for work in the early afternoon, according to Delilah, so that was his window of opportunity. He left his car at the house, walking to Delilah's. It was a twenty-five-minute walk compared to the eight-minute drive to get there. But he couldn't risk his car being seen.

He arrived, inwardly cringing as he made his way towards the back of the house. Tossing his black hoodie over his head. Delilah's house was a white, one-story bungalow similar to his aunts. He figured not having stairs or an attic would make the search quick. Surveying his surroundings, he pulled out a heavy-duty paper clip and one of his aunt's bobby pins, folding the paperclip into an L shape and sticking it through the key slot. He unfolded the bobby pin, sticking it above the paperclip. Maneuvering them both until he heard the clicks. He went inside, removing his hood, he took soft steps, listening for any sounds of movement. He observed that neither Delilah nor her mother's car was outside. Slowly, he entered the house, removed his hood, and stepped quietly to listen for any sudden movements. Hearing none, he began his search for the book.

He first searched the living room, flipping through different books on the coffee table. Then scanning the bookshelf for any signs of a red book. He headed down the narrow hallway where the bedrooms were, checking Delilah's first. He moved at a slower pace searching through her things, to ensure that he didn't leave any trace of someone being in the house. He checked her drawers, the closet, and even under her mattress. But nothing. He went to her mother's bedroom, doing a repeat of the same places. He checked the closet last, but still no sign of any red book.

He began to pace back and forth, becoming both agitated and racked with guilt from having to do this. He took a deep breath and thought about where a parent would keep something they didn't want other people to find, not even their own children. He remembered how Hank used to hide his cigar boxes from them when they were younger. Jackson found them inside an encyclopedia with the pages hollowed out. Jackson decided to go back to the bookcase in the living room. Starting with the random books first, then moving on to the others. Mostly romance novels with dust jackets. That's when he found it. Hidden between the hollowed-out pages of a Nora Jones book, was a small red 4x7 book. With the eye symbol. Just like Bryce said. Jackson grabbed the book, putting the novel back in its place and hurrying out of the house as quickly as he could. The only thing left to do was go to Bryce and finish this once and for all.

***

He went back to Carrie's house to get his car and headed to the spot where Bryce took him to meet up. When he arrived, looking upon the hill where the bunker was, Bryce stood by the metal door giving Jackson a mock salute. His gesture, carrying a smugness to it. Jackson felt a chill creep up his spine. Suppressing a shudder he headed down the hill, with the book in hand.

"I must say, I'm surprised you came so soon. That was quick. That Delilah sure didn't waste any time with you, did she?" Bryce said with a smirk.

Jackson's jaw tightened, he slammed the book against Bryce's chest. "You keep her name out of your mouth and you leave my aunt and her house alone. We're done here." He turned to head back up the hill.

"Not so fast city boy. I never said we were done."

Jackson halted, turning around. "No. I did what you asked!"

"Yes, but this is just the first half of what I need," Bryce said, moving closer towards him. "You see Jackson, freedom comes with a price."

Two more shifters came from behind the bunker. Stephan, and the other boy from the night at the market.

"What the hell is going on?" Jackson questioned, clenching his fists as Stephan sized him up.

"Jackson, relax," Bryce said. "I told you, I'm not the enemy. I'm doing what needs to be done. What I am chosen to do. Have you ever heard of Akinde?"

Jackson didn't respond, he was too focused on the other two, ready to end whatever trouble they were waiting to start.

"Akinde was a slave burned alive in 1648 in Germany. Accused of being a witch, and she was." Bryce circled Jackson, cradling the book at his waist. "But before she died, she cursed the men that burned her. And their children, grandchildren… you get the idea. That curse is why we exist today." He continued. "The spirit of Akinde is the key to giving us true power. With her spirit at our control, shifters can rule the world. But her spirit first required the blood sacrifice of the cursed. As you know, the feys. But she also needs a living body to take her final form… the living body of a descendant."

Bryce held up the book, his left eyebrow raising slightly. He didn't need to say a word. Jackson, gaping at Bryce with a menacing look, already knew.

"You go anywhere near Delilah and I will kill you myself," Jackson muttered.

"You see, that's why I need you," Bryce said eagerly. "Delilah has to come here at her own free will. And you will bring her to me."

"Does the council know about this?"

"The council can't do a thing. As far as they know we're just a bunch of bottom feeders who know a few magic tricks. You bring them here or get them involved in any way, and all this disappears. They'll never believe you." Bryce let out a bitter laugh.

"Take the house! This isn't worth it anymore! I'm done! Stay away from me, my aunt, and Delilah!"

"Oh, you poor fool." Bryce titled his head. "You still think you have a choice?"

The anger swelling in Jackson had reached its peak. He punched Bryce in the face, his knuckles cracking the bridge of his nose. Bryce recoiled, catching the blood as it ran down his nose.

Stephan and the other shifter immediately shifted, So, did Jackson.

"Back down, let him go!" Bryce ordered.

Jackson shifted back, taking off up the hill and back to his car.

"He'll be back." Said Bryce, wiping the blood from his nose with a satisfying grin.

CHAPTER 9

Jackson arrived back at his aunt's house, as he pulled up he saw Delilah's car parked, and her sitting on the front steps. She had on the same clothes he saw her in the day before, and there was something hollow about her appearance. She looked at him as he got out, her eyes sunken and dejected.

"Delilah, what are you doing here?" He asked. "I thought you were at school."

She looked up at him, her lips were dry and there were was dry ash on her cheeks. She had been crying. "I came by, but your aunt said you were out, so I waited for you." She said, her voice low and raspy.

"What happened? What's wrong?" He took a seat next to her, putting his arm around her shoulder.

"Everything." She placed her head on his shoulder. "I just want to rest. I'm so tired." She said.

Burdened by his guilt, a weight settled on his heart. He held her closer. "Delilah, I want to talk to you about something."

"Actually, me too." She said. "That's why I'm here. Can we go inside?"

"Yeah, come on." They stood and headed into the house and up to Jackson's room.

She sat down at the edge of the bed, her hands resting in her lap. He took a seat next to her.

"Can I ask you something?" She said.

"Yeah?"

"What do you know about your father?"

His eyebrows drew together. "Uh, well, I know he died before I was born. My stepdad never talked about what he did for a living. Just that he invested in a bunch of stock and left me a trust fund. Why do you ask?"

Delilah twiddled her thumbs, taking in a breath. "There's something I need to show you." She reached into her pocket, and took out the photo of her and Silas, handing it to him.

He looked at it. "That's my father. Why do you have a picture of my father and…" He squinted, "Some baby."

Delilah looked up into his eyes, letting out a huff of discomfort. "Jackson, that baby is me. I'm your sister."

There was a moment of silence, so uncomfortable that Delilah's stomach heaved at the memory of her trying to kiss him.

Jackson bit his bottom lip, staring blankly at the wall ahead. Suddenly, every encounter, every feeling he had for her came full circle. It all made sense now. The strong connection they shared wasn't romantic at all. She and him were blood. Torn apart by human selfishness but destined to be brought back together through their beastly spirits. He took in and let out a deep breath. His elbows rested on his thighs, he turned to Delilah.

"We almost kissed." He said.

Delilah's eyes grew wide, embarrassment lacerating her insides. Then they both burst into laughter, turning a moment of humiliation and shock into a moment of hilarity.

"Oh God, why are we laughing?" Delilah said, her fingers pressed against her eyes. "There is nothing funny about any of this."

"I honestly don't know. This is a lot." He said, trying to suppress his laughter. "How do you even know if this is really true? It's just a photo."

"My mother told me to stay away from you after you left yesterday. I got angry and told her I wouldn't. That's when she showed me this photo and told me everything."

Jackson looked at the picture still in his hands. "You were a cute baby." He smiled at her.

"Apparently our father didn't think so. He abandoned me and my momma a month after I was born." Her eyes lowered, the pain of it all coming back to her. "I don't know what hurts the most. My mother and fake father lying to me my whole life, my real father abandoning me and giving everything to his son like I didn't even exist, or the humiliation of unknowingly having a crush on my brother."

He squeezed her hand. "If I could take back what my father did, I would. I spent my entire life alone, wondering if I had any real family out there. People who would love and understand me like Hank and his kids never could. Then I found my aunt and my life changed. And now, my life is forever changed because of you. And don't feel bad about the crush thing. That's our parent's shame to carry. Not ours. We didn't know."

A smile lit up on Delilah's face. "So, where do we go from here?"

"We start over." He held out his other hand, "Nice to meet you, sis." He smiled.

She accepted his handshake, as he pulled her into a hug. A joy welled from within his heart as he held her close. His joy was short-lived, as he thought about Bryce. His throat tightened, wondering how he'd ever have the heart to tell Delilah about it all. His need to protect her from Bryce was more crucial now that she was family. But Bryce still needed Jackson to get to her, so if he kept her away, things would be fine.

"So, what was it that you wanted to talk about?" She asked as they broke their embrace.

He looked at her with pressed lips. "It was nothing. Don't worry about it." He said.

"Oh, well I'm gonna head home to shower & change. I'm calling in sick so no work today. Let's hang out when I come back."

"Yeah, sure."

They left his room, he walked her to the door and waited as she left. He headed back upstairs, pondering a plan to get Delilah and his aunt out of town. If the Barbeau family was going to take Carrie's house, she'd have to move anyway. He thought of asking her to come to Chicago. She could stay in his cabin and be safe there. She had spent her entire life in Louisiana, and he knew she'd never want to leave her bakery behind. But he had to try. As for Delilah, he'd have to tell her about the book, and Bryce's plan. And if she didn't hate him, maybe she would leave too.

CHAPTER 10

With their newfound kinship, Delilah wanted to show him all the things she could never share with anyone else, growing up as an only child. She wasn't the type to make friends, and the rigidity in her mother's parenting made the few friends Delilah did manage to have, hard to keep. Being with Jackson was the first time she could ever get close to someone without feeling like they wanted something from her. A spell to cheat on a test, a potion to clear up acne. It was always something with others. But with Jackson, she felt that there were no expectations, no conditions. Just a genuine bond.

She took him to Coushatta Mountain. The highest natural summit in all of Louisiana, located about thirty minutes from town. With an elevation of 535 feet above sea level, it was perfect for hiking, climbing, and the perfect getaway for shifters. When they arrived, she led him down the red trail where oak trees stretched for what seemed liked miles. Trees at least a hundred feet tall.

"I've never seen trees this big," Jackson said, gazing up at them as he and Delilah walked. "From here it kind of looks like they reach the sky almost."

"Well, we'll just have to see for ourselves," Delilah said.

Delilah took his hand, pulled out her necklace, and once again the earth ceased around them. Delilah walked up to one of the trees, placing her hands against the bark.

"What are you doing?" Jackson asked.

"*Kewaa patentibus.*" She whispered, slowly moving her hands away. Suddenly, small crevices appeared, vertically up the bark. Delilah clutched the small open splits and began to climb.

"Well, don't just stand there, silly," she teased. "Let's go!" She quickly moved up the oak tree.

He followed behind as they made their way to the top, the warm smell of wood held a strong tinge of vanilla. Getting stronger as they got further up. They reached the thick branches, pulling themselves up and sitting on branches strong enough to hold them. Delilah swung her legs, inhaling through her nose as the stiff air sat on their skin. Jackson took in the panoramic view of the scenery.

"This is amazing." He said, in awe of how the broad pine colored leaves from all the other trees complimented the landscape of the county.

"This is where I came last night, after the fight with my momma," Delilah said, holding on to the bark as she stood upon the branch. She dug into her pocket, pulling out a small handful of a sand-like substance.

"Whoa!" he shouted. "Why are you standing? You'll hurt yourself!"

"No, I won't." She walked along the branch, with her arms out, balancing her step. She mumbled a spell, holding out her hand and blowing the sand into the air and lifting her foot away from the branch.

"Delilah be careful!" Jackson yelled out, reaching out for her.

But she didn't fall. She slid across the air like it was ice. She did a short twirl, holding out her arms in his direction.

"Come on." She urged.

His eyes gleamed with surprise. "No way." He said, his eyes fixated on her feet.

"It's safe. I promise." She gestures for him to come to her, with her hands out.

Jackson lifts and stands on the branch, moving slowly as he moves his foot forward. He takes a step, and the air is solid. His legs weakened as he tried to maintain balance. Delilah slid over to him, taking ahold of his arms and pulling him out further.

"This is wild. I'm impressed, but also kind of terrified." He said.

"I've done this plenty of times. But this is the first time I've done it with another person. So if you fall, my apologies in advance."

"Delilah that's not funny!"

She laughed. "I'm kidding! It's rock-solid, see." She jumped, slamming her foot against the invisible surface. "I've always wanted to go ice skating. Somewhere cold, like Michigan." She said, gliding them around in circles.

"Then you'd like Chicago. Illinois gets pretty cold, and our winters are long." He said.

"Any place sounds better than here." She lowered her eyes, gazing down at the world below. "For the first time in my life, I feel like I can just be myself with someone. When I dated Stephan, it never felt genuine. And whenever I make friends it never lasts. But having a brother, it just feels right." She smiled.

Jackson's guilt made it's way back. "Speaking of Chicago, I was thinking maybe we could take a trip? You, me, and Aunt Carrie?"

"I don't know, school isn't even out yet."

"You're about to graduate anyway, what's a few weeks gonna hurt?"

"Jackson, it's too soon. I can't just leave town on a whim like that."

He stood still, his grip getting tighter. "Please?"

Her eyes squinted. "Why so urgent? Are you tired of the south already?" She teased.

"No, it's not that." He frowned. "Delilah, I-"

Her cellphone rang, diverting her attention as she dug into her back pocket and pulled it out. "It's my momma."

"How is your phone ringing right now?"

Delilah huffed, "My time stopper comes with an annoying little parental control. My mother can reach me if it's an emergency. Or if she just wants to be annoying." She answered it, "Hello?"

"Where are you?" Mary screamed into her ear. "I called your job and they said you didn't come in!"

"I'm out with Jackson, why are you yelling?"

"He's with you? Thank God! You both need to get back right now. It's Ms. Lakota. Her house caught fire. She's here at the hospital. It's not looking good."

Delilah froze, her face wore a blank expression.

"What is it?" Jackson asked.

"We're coming now," Delilah told her mother, hanging up the phone. She looked up at Jackson who was waiting for her to tell him what was going on. "We've gotta head back. Your aunt is in the hospital."

His blood ran cold. He let go of Delilah and headed back to the tree, hurrying down the branches.

"Jackson, wait!" She went after him, restarting her clock as they left the park and headed back to town.

***

They arrived at Mercy hospital and headed straight through the ER wing, to room 103 where Carrie was being treated. As they got closer, Mary came from inside the room, spotting them immediately. Her eyes welled up as she looked at him, then Delilah. Giving a slight nod as she closed the door. Terror overtook his face, pain gripped his chest.

"Jackson... I think you should wait in the lobby." Mary told him.

But it was too late, he had already shoved past her to get inside. There in the bed, lied Aunt Carrie. The left side of her arm, covered in third-degree burns. He squeezed his eyes shut as they flooded with tears. Delilah came in after him, her hands clasped over her mouth.

"She passed away about fifteen minutes ago. Smoke inhalation." Mary told them.

"How did this happen?" Jackson uttered, standing next to the bed.

"We aren't sure yet. The firefighters think it was electrical. A bad socket. She was in the bathroom when they found her. They said she was screaming about the door being locked, but when they checked, it wasn't."

An alarm rang in his mind. Bryce. Anger seared through him. He pressed his palms against his eyes, trying to calm himself down.

"I think we should give him a moment," Mary said, taking Delilah out of the room to wait in the lobby.

Jackson reached down and grabbed Carrie's burned hand. She looked so peaceful, as tragic as her final moments were.

"I should've been there. This is all my fault. I'm so sorry Aunt Carrie." He whispered. A sob escaped him, as he wiped his tears with shaking hands. "I won't let him get away with this, I promise."

CHAPTER 11

Delilah and Jackson sat in the lobby, as she held his hand trying to comfort him. His grief, dragging her down with him. Slouched back in his seat, a million thoughts ran through his head at once. His only priority now was finding Bryce.

"I should take you back to my house, you need to rest," Delilah suggested.

"It's my fault she's dead." He said.

"No, don't say that. It's nobody's fault. It was an accident."

Jackson turned to her, he knew it was time to finally tell her the truth. "I stole the book."

"What are you talking about?"

"From your house. I broke in and stole the spellbook. I gave it to Bryce. Now my aunt is dead because…" He took in a deep breath.

"Wait, I don't' understand…"

"I'm sorry, I have to go." He got up and headed out of the lobby.

She got up, following after him. "Jackson, wait up!" She caught up to him, pulling at his arm. "Stop! You need to explain what's going on!" She demanded.

He faced her, his head hung in shame. "My aunt got a letter last week. The Barbeau's were going to take her home. Bryce came by the bakery and told me that if I got him a spellbook from your house, that they wouldn't take it." He began to tear up again, watching her expression turn from concern to confusion. "I gave him the book, but he said it wasn't enough. He wanted me to bring you to him as a sacrifice for a ritual. But I told him no. I would never do that to you, I swear." He continued.

"You… broke into my house?" Disappointment hung from her eyes.

"I never meant for any of this to happen. I told him to stay away from you. And now he killed my aunt. I have to fix this. I'm so sorry Delilah. I'm going to find Bryce." He said, turning to leave the parking lot.

"Then I'm going with you. She called out to him, jogging to catch up. "Whatever he's trying to do, he won't get far. He's not the first asshole to abuse magic or take advantage of people to get what he wants. And I'm sure he won't be the last. I'm not afraid of him."

"No! This is what he wants. He said the ritual won't work unless you come at your own will. I made the mistake of giving him that book. I won't let him take the only family I have left."

He tried to walk away but she ran in front of him, pushing her hands against his chest. "Last I checked, I'm the one who knows magic. And I'm the oldest, so technically you have to listen to me." She said with a raised brow.

"We don't have time for this." He huffed. "I said you weren't going anywhere near that place and I meant it."

"So, let me guess your plan. You're going to confront Bryce, his crew, and risk getting killed, right?"

"I guess so. At least you'll be safe from him."

"How do you know that? What makes you think he won't find other ways to come after me? Unless somebody stops him, I'll never be safe. And neither will you."

"So what do we do then?"

"Well, we have to get that book back." She said, rubbing her chin. "I have an idea. We could use my time stopper. Do you know where Bryce could be?"

He shrugged. "There's a bunker a few miles away. That's where we met up, but I don't know if he's there now. Give me the clock and I'll go."

"Only a witch can use an enchanted clock. You have to take me with you."

"No. It's too risky." Jackson shook his head, turning around to walk away.

Delilah stopped him again, "Wait, I have a potion we can use. It's a shifting potion. I can alter my outer appearance to match yours, and it'll mask my scent temporarily. They won't know it's me."

He stood there, staring at her with his arms folded. "You don't have to do this. It's not your mess to clean up."

"It is now. And this is what siblings do. They look out for each other, even when the other does something stupid. So I'm going whether you like it or not."

He wrapped an arm around her shoulders and pulled her close, gently rubbing her arm. "Alright. Let's get that book."

***

They stopped by Delilah's house to get the shifting potion, and Jackson drove them to the abandoned bunker in her car. They parked a quarter of a mile away to avoid either of their scents being picked up by Bryce or the others. Delilah pulled out the small bottle, like the one that held the blue liquid. But this one was red.

"Are you sure this plan will work?" Jackson asked.

"I don't see why it won't." She unscrewed the cap, reaching over and plucking a small strand of hair from his head.

"Ouch!" He rubbed his head. "A heads up would've been nice. Why can't you just use the time stopper before you get inside anyway?"

"I can't overlap a complex potion like this with an enchantment. So it's either one or the other. Bryce is older and a bit more experienced, he could have a counter-charm around the building. I think the potion is our best bet. I just have to play it cool. Wear off the charm in just enough time to grab the book and use my clock."

She slid the strand of hair into the bottle, and they both watched as it disintegrated into the liquid. "This is gonna get weird, so don't freak out." She told him, tilting her head back and placing three drops on her tongue.

Jackson watched with wide eyes as Delilah's jet black hair turned to chestnut brown curls. Her skin, even her clothes, now identical to his. She pulled down the visor mirror, running her palms across her face. Her mouth formed into a grin.

Jackson poked her face with his index finger. "Oh my God."

"Cool isn't it? I know it's a lot to take in but give it a few minutes. You'll get used to it." She closed the visor, "So, to make sure we're on the same page, you wait outside. Don't come in after me unless it's been over fifteen minutes. Besides, if he picks up your scent, he'll just assume it's me."

"Got it."

They got out of the car and headed for the hill. Delilah sped up, with Jackson staying a short distance behind. He waited outside, keeping an eye on his surroundings as she went to the bunker, scoping out the area before going inside. When she opened the metal door, Bryce stood there, startling her.

"Geez, you should learn to announce yourself instead of sneaking up on people," Delilah said.

"Jackson, I wasn't expecting you. And I see you've come empty-handed." Bryce said, peering into his eyes.

Delilah straightened her shoulders, reminding herself that she wasn't in her own body. At least not on the outside.

"I wanted to talk to you. About joining." She said.

He squinted, "This is unexpected. But, as I said before, we are a brotherhood. Good to see you've come to your senses."

She lifted her chin, trying to match his masculine demeanor. "Well, my circumstances have changed."

"Why yes, I heard about the fire. You have my condolences." The evil gleam in his eyes made Delilah's skin crawl.

"Appreciate it." She replied, trying to hide her disgust.

"Now, I still expect you to bring us the girl. That won't be a problem, will it?"

"Not at all. I've decided that things between Delilah and I ain't…" Her accent began to slip through. "I mean, we're not working out. Turns out she's not really my type. So, it won't be a problem."

"Well then, welcome."

Bryce led her to the stone door, and down the stairs into his lair. Her belly cramped as there was nothing but darkness, and the flames of candles illuminating all around. When they got to the bottom, the candles burned brighter, and she could see the area more clearly. Stephan sat in a corner with a bottle of beer in his hands. The space was damp, the smell of mold being masked with an aroma spell.

"What's he doing down here?" Stephan stood up, his eyes dead set on Delilah.

"Relax Stephan. Jackson is one of us now." Bryce said with a solid grip on Delilah's shoulder. "Isn't that right Jackson?" He said, with a grin.

"Yeah." She muttered, her hands becoming clammy.

"And you trust this guy?" Stephan said.

Bryce walked over to Stephan, clasping his hand around Stephan's throat. "Don't you ever question me." He said through gritted teeth.

Veins emerged in Stephan's neck as he choked through his words. Delilah gazed around while they were both distracted. Over on the far left, was a small table. Placed on a book lift, was the Book of Gods' spellbook. She took small steps away, glancing back at the boys. Stephan rubbing his throat, coughing and Bryce walking back over to her. She needed to wait for the perfect time to make her way towards the table to grab the book, switch back to her own body, and stop the clock in time without the others catching on.

"Jackson, you came at the perfect time I must say. The full moon is tonight. Our open window to complete the ritual." Bryce said. "The sooner the better. We need Delilah tonight. Akinde is waiting."

Delilah's throat tightened, slowly making small steps backward. "How do you even know she's a descendant? What if you're wrong?"

Bryce let out a sinister chuckle. "Do you think I'm stupid? Are you insulting my intelligence city boy?"

"No, I wasn't. I was just- "

"You think we're all just mindless hicks down here in good ole' Louisiana, don't you?" Bryce drew closer as Delilah's heart thumped against her ribcage.

"No. I don't think that at all."

Delilah's back pressed against the table, knocking the book off the lift. One hand moved towards the book, the other slowly reaching for her necklace. But her eyes were still glued on Bryce. His expression sending a shiver down her spine. This was her only chance.

Bryce was now, inches away from her face. "The only stupid one here is you. Delilah."

In a split second, she started to transform back into herself, grabbing hold of the book and preparing to stop her clock as the rest of the shifting potion wore off. Bryce's eyes grew wide as he clutched her neck with one hand, snatching the necklace from her neck and tossing it on the ground. He stepped on it, shattering the glass and tiny handles. Delilah kicked him in the crotch, which didn't halt him long enough as he tossed her to the other side of the room, sending her slamming against the cold, stone wall.

"Jackson!" She screamed for him, crawling toward the stairs.

"Go take care of him," Bryce ordered. Stephan sprung up, darting up the stairs and out of the bunker.

Delilah regained her footing, making a run for it towards the stairs but Bryce swung his hand, pulling her back with force. She yelped in pain as the rigid stone wall sent sharp pain down her left side. He went towards her, as she lay there, her hand pressed against her side. He kneeled, smirking at her.

"Don't make me hurt you again. Akinde needs her host's body in good condition if you don't mind."

Delilah put her hands on his face and uttered *kewaa patentibus* spell. A large gash whipped across his face as he screamed out in agony. Blood ran from his wound.

"You little bitch!" He back-handed her.

She held her face, crying with trembling hands, huddling against the wall. With her clock destroyed, the few spells she knew wouldn't be enough to get her out of this. Bryce was too strong. She had no way out. Her only hope now was Jackson.

CHAPTER 12

Back outside, Jackson waited off to the side of the bunker anticipating her return. It hadn't been fifteen minutes yet, but his heart was racing with every passing second. Dread twisted in his gut as he sensed something was wrong. He heard the metal door opening, so he rushed over assuming it was Delilah. But out walked Stephan, his muscles tensed. His eyes narrow, cold, and hard.

"Where is she?" Jackson questioned, clenching his fists at his sides.

"She's Bryce's problem now." Stephan took one last swig from his beer bottle and sent it shattering to the ground. "And you're mine." He shifted into the beast, charging at Jackson with barred teeth.

Jackson turned swiftly, dodging his attack. Stephan circled back around, lunging at Jackson who had him by the neck. Stephan used his hind legs to kick Jackson off him. Jackson landed on a pipe that stuck out from underneath the ground, impairing him. Stephan now had the upper hand, clawing at Jackson's torso. Jackson bit his arm sending Stephan recoiling back. Both suffering from injuries shifted back into their human form to heal.

Breathless and exhausted, Jackson needed to end this fight and get to Delilah. He peered over to his right, where shards of glass from Stephan's beer bottle lay on the ground. Stephan cocking his neck to the side and grinding his teeth, shifted again, and lunged. Jackson grabbed the glass, stabbing Stephan in the chest on impact. A loud whimper emerged as Stephan fell over. Jackson watched in shock as Stephan bled out, taking his last, gasping breaths.

Jackson dropped the glass, quickly standing to his feet. Stephan was now back in his human form. His lifeless body huddled and frail. Jackson could feel his legs numbing at the sight, but he had no time to deal with the trauma response of killing someone. Delilah was still in trouble. He ran inside the bunker, slamming against the stone door as he called for her.

"Delilah!" He screamed. "Bryce let her go!" He kicked at the door, knowing it was no use but he couldn't give up on her.

Bryce looked up to the top of the stairs, grunting in frustration that Jackson was still alive. "That idiot Stephan." He rolled his eyes. "I always knew he was useless."

Delilah, now chained to the wall, begged Bryce to spare him. "Please, don't hurt him." She cried.

"I won't. Not yet anyway. I'll save him for after the ritual. That way you, well, Akinde can kill him instead."

"You're a monster! You'll never get away with this!" Delilah screamed, yanking at the chains.

"Actually, I will." Bryce glanced at the watch on his wrist. "In about an hour when the sun sets." A malicious scowl etched across his face.

He opened the door with a swift motion of his hand, sending Jackson flying down the stairs. The stone door slammed shut. Before Jackson could raise to his feet, Bryce grabbed the spellbook, holding it open with his hand outstretched.

"*accipere anụ ọhịa!*" Bryce pronounced with ease.

Jackson felt his chest caving in, and a white haze emerged from within him. It swiveled around the air, flying between the pages of the spellbook as Bryce closed it.

"What did you do to me!" He yelled, momentarily paralyzed.

"I removed the soul of the beast from within you. I have Delilah's. Now I have yours. You're powerless." Bryce laughed mirthlessly, tossing the book back on the table.

Thick vines burst through the concrete floors, wrapping around Jackson's arms and legs as he tried to release himself from their powerful grip. The thorns pricking his skin like tiny razor blades. The vines tugged his wrists and legs like steel wire cables. Pinned to the floor, his skin burning red with anger. Bryce walked up to him, kneeling and taunting Jackson with that devilish grin and those heinous green eyes.

"As much as I would love to kill you, it'll be more fun watching Akinde do it when she returns. "Bryce said. "But torturing you one finger at a time until the full moon rises should be fun."

"Leave him alone!" Delilah screamed.

"I know you started that fire. "Said, Jackson." And I swear on my family's graves I will kill you before the sun rises."

Bryce just stared at him with pressed lips, giving him a pat on the shoulder. "Sure you will."

He got up and headed to the table, picking up his blade. He twirled it in his hands, still covered in dried blood from the last sacrifice. Delilah pleaded with him to not hurt Jackson, yanking away at the chains that bound her. Bryce approached Jackson with the blade, kneeling beside him.

"What do you say we welcome our queen Akinde with a proper greeting?" Bryce said, raising the blade to Jackson's face.

"Get away from me you psycho!" Jackson jerked his head away as Bryce gripped his chin, pulling the edge of the blade to his skin.

Delilah's eyes bulged as she watched Bryce slice the letters of Akinde's name into Jackson's skin as he screeched out in agony. The sight of his blood sent her into a state of fit of rage.

"Stop it!" She shouted, her wrists bruising as she tried to free herself.

Another slice against Jackson's skin, more blood running. More screaming. Delilah trembled, her skin prickling with fear as she began to panic. The walls around them shook, bits of stone crumbling from the ceiling.

Bryce halted, looking at her. "What the hell is happening?" He ran over to her, holding the blade against her cheek as he aggressively held her face.

The force within her becoming stronger as the stone began to crumble. The floor, breaking apart and rising up. The vines that held Jackson down detached from their roots. He snapped himself free as the ceiling began to cave in. A huge chunk of stone fell from above, striking Bryce in the head and knocking him unconscious.

"Jackson, get the book!"

He ran to grab the book from the table, dodging the chunks that fell from the ceiling as Delilah, now free from the wall, ran to him. She grabbed the book, frantically flipping the pages until she found the one. The transportation spell.

"*evanescet!*" Delilah shouted.

Locking arms, she and Jackson were thrust from inside the imploding bunker to the middle of the road. Her car still sat a few feet away from where they parked. Taking a second to catch their breath, Delilah ran her palm across his face where he was cut.

"Are you okay?" She asked.

"I'm fine. Are you?"

"Yeah, just shaken up that's all." She hugged him.

They got out of the road and went to her car.

"You think he's dead?" Jackson asked as Delilah padded and dug into her jeans pocket for her keys.

She blew a sigh of relief, pulling them out and starting the car. "I hope so. But I'm not sticking around to find out."

CHAPTER 13

Jackson sat at the kitchen table as Delilah cleaned his deep cuts with a warm cloth. She dipped her fingers in a small bowl of a loose clay substance, smearing small amounts over the open gashes. He hissed from the sting.

"Just give it a second." She said, using the cloth to wipe her fingers. "The stinging will go away. Then you'll be good as new."

"What happened down in that bunker… where did that come from?" Jackson asked.

Delilah's eyes lowered, "It happens sometimes when I get angry. I can't control it, but it never gets that bad. I guess seeing Bryce hurt you, and a mix of my emotions from being chained up, it triggered me."

"Well, you saved us. I guess those triggers come in handy then."

"We got lucky. If we didn't have the book to get us out we'd probably be dead. I could've killed us." She walked over to the sink, leaning against the counter. "When I was five, I was kidnapped by a cult. The leader was a friend of my momma. Just like Bryce, they wanted to sacrifice me to bring Akinde back. But I killed them."

Jackson looked at her, his eyebrows raised with a blank expression.

"I don't remember what happened. But I remember almost drowning. And bloody dead bodies floating around me. You see, I'm not just a descendant. I was born during the harvest full moon. The same as Akinde. I have certain abilities that mirror those of hers when she was alive. Abilities that witches haven't seen for centuries." Her voice became thick with fear. "There will always be another cult. Another Bryce. I'll never truly be safe as long as I'm alive."

Jackson got up, walking over to her. "You'll be safe with me. Besides, I've got the brawn and you've got the brains. And the spells. Together we can get out of anything." He placed his arm around her.

"We do make a good team, huh." She smiled, which quickly turned into a frown. "But after tonight, I don't think you'll ever be safe with me around. I think you should leave in the morning."

"What? No. If I leave, you're coming with me." He pulled her into a tight hug. "It doesn't matter who comes for you, or when. We'll be ready every time."

Something about his embrace always made her feel reassured. Like there was hope, even when she felt none.

"I'll leave with you then. We can go tomorrow."

"Are you sure?"

"I'm sure. I'll explain everything to my momma when she gets home. She'll be upset, but she'll get over it eventually." Delilah took a deep breath, running her hands over her face. "I'm gonna go grab some Tylenol from the bathroom. Then we can discuss what's next."

"Sounds good."

Delilah began to leave the kitchen, he took hold of her arm.

"Wait." He said to her in a solemn voice.

She turned back and could see in his eyes that there was something troubling him. "What is it?" She asked.

He walked back over to the chair to sit. He slumped, staring down at his feet. As he tried to gather the words he needed to express this affliction that sat on his heart, she walked over and stood next to him.

"I killed Stephan." He uttered.

Delilah had already figured that out when he arrived inside the bunker to save her. But hearing him say it out loud, was the confirmation they both needed to know that it was real. She stood behind him, leaning down with her chest against his back as she wrapped her arms around him.

"It's okay." She said, thinking about her past, and what happened to Bryce in the bunker. "We all do things we aren't proud of sometimes. It's not your fault." She reassured him.

"I've never killed anyone before. I don't regret it, and I would do it again if it meant saving you or anyone else I care about. But…" He forced down a sick feeling. "I still feel like a monster."

"No, you're not. And neither am I. People like Bryce, Stephan and the ones who kidnapped me when I was little, they're the real monsters. Not us. Not you." She squeezed him tighter, pressing the side of her face against his.

He placed his hand on her am, "I'm so glad you came into my life. No mater the circumstances. I'm glad we found each other." He said.

"Me too."

She left him in the kitchen and headed to the bathroom. Turning on the faucet, she splashed cold water on her face, raking her fingers through her hair. She stared at her reflection in the mirror, the images of the crumbling bunker flashing through her head. She opened the cabinet, grabbing the bottle of pain killers. As she closed it, her cellphone rang. She dropped the bottle in the sink, digging into her back pocket to get her phone. It was a call from her mother. After what had just happened, hearing her mother's voice would put her at ease.

"Hey, momma." She answered.

"I'm sorry, Momma can't come to the phone right now. She's a bit tied up at the moment."

Delilah's stomach dropped, adrenaline pumping through her at the sound of his voice. "Bryce... where is my momma?" her voice trembled.

"She's in the trunk of her car, on her way to what was my bunker before you destroyed it. And unless you want to find her dead and burned to a crisp, I suppose you get moving. The night isn't over yet. I'll be waiting."

He hung up, Delilah ran back to the kitchen. "He's got my momma!"

Jackson sprung up from his chair. "What happened?"

"Bryce just called from my momma's phone. He took her! He said he'll kill her if we don't meet him back at the hill!"

"We can't go back there without a plan." Jackson said.

"I don't care! We'll figure it out on the way! He may have survived the bunker, but he'll still be too weakened to use all of his powers for now. So we have an advantage." She grabbed the spellbook from the table. "Before we go I need to restore the souls of the beasts in us."

She opened the book, flipping to the page that held their beastly spirits. "*accipere anu ọhịa!*"

The white haze emerged from the pages, whirling around in the air before uniting with their human bodies. A surge of fresh energy filled them, their blood pumping fast through their veins. Jackson looked at his arms, clenching his hands into fists as his muscles tensed.

"Ah, feels good to be back." He said.

*** *** ***

They drove back to the hill, running towards the demolished remains of the bunker where Bryce stood, bruised, bloodied, and waiting. Their minds too muddled to come up with a solid plan that wouldn't backfire. Their only priority was saving Mary, and the rest was in the hands of fate. But they wouldn't surrender or let Bryce get away without a fight. Next to Bryce, Mary was tied from the chest down to an old flag pole, her mouth bound with tape. Doused in gasoline, the left side of her face stained with blood from being struck with a blunt object while getting into her car at the end of her shift. Jackson stood next to her, holding a lit torch.

"Momma!" Delilah cried out to her as they ran in her direction.

"Don't you even think about it!" Bryce stopped them before they could get any closer. "And if you even think about shifting, she goes up in flames." He threatened, holding the torch inches away from Mary's feet. He eyed the book that Delilah held underneath her arm. "The book, give it to me."

"Don't do it!" Jackson told her.

She looked at her mother, whose muffled screams felt like a knife to the heart. Delilah's temples throbbed as her skin felt like burning asphalt. Thunder rumbled, large bolts of lightning lit up the sky as the ground began to rumble. "If I do, let her go." She demanded.

"She's not the one I want," Bryce said. "But it's your choice. Give me the book, or she dies."

Even with the book, Delilah knew he still needed her body to complete the ritual before dawn. But she had to save her mother first. The only thing that mattered at the moment. She inched closer, keeping her eyes on the flames of the torch.

"That's close enough. Toss it." Bryce said as she stood about eight feet away.

She flung the book on the ground at his feet, he reached down to grab it. In the split second that he was distracted, Jackson shifted, charging at Bryce, and tackling him. The torch flew out of his hands and rolled away, igniting a fire in the grass nearby. Jackson had Bryce pinned, as Delilah ran to her mother, removing the tape from her mouth. Bryce leered into Jackson's eyes, a smirk formed as reached from the waistband of his pants, pulling out his blade, and stabbing Jackson in the chest. Jackson let out a whimper, shifting back into his human form as Bryce kicked him off.

"Jackson!" Delilah screamed.

With wide eyes, her heart wrenched at the sight of Bryce hovering over Jackson, impaling him a second time in the chest. The blood dripped from the knife, Bryce turned to Delilah, the scowl on his face was like something out of a nightmare. The world around her went still, her jaw went slack. There was so much blood, as Jackson lay there, trembling and clinging to life. Her pupils constricted as Bryce's arm swung forward, the blade aimed for her heart. Her mother's screams drowned out behind her as the knife got closer. Until it stopped. Two inches away from her chest. Bryce's eyes grew wide as he watched the knife hanging in mid-air, slowly crumble into pieces. He began to float upwards, losing control of his arms and legs as they went numb. The wind picked up, blowing out the fire that formed in the grass around them. Thunder roared and the lightning bolts struck nearby trees. The ropes that bound Mary snapped, releasing her from the pole. Bryce's eyes turned from terror to wonder, as he watched Delilah wreak havoc. Her powers reining beautifully in chaos. He let out an ominous yet satisfying chuckle.

"Akinde, my queen." He uttered before a huge hole ripped through his chest. His blood splattered into the air like raindrops.

His body hit the ground. The thunder and lightening stopped, Delilah snapped out of her hypnotic state. Staring at Bryce's dead body, the shock of what was happening kicked in as she heard her mother yelling her name.

"Delilah!" Mary called out to her, as she kneeled next to Jackson, holding his head up with her hand pressed against his wound as he bled to death. Choking on his own blood.

Delilah ran to him, dropping to her knees as her eyes filled with tears. "Jackson don't die! Please!" She begged, holding his face with her palms. "Momma do something! We need to get him to a hospital!" She pleaded.

Mary looked into her eyes, not wanting to be the one to state the obvious. She placed her hand on top of Delilah's. "We wouldn't make it in time. It's too late."

"No! There has to be something!" Delilah protested, clenching his bloody shirt as her tears fell. "We can use the transportation spell!"

"It still wouldn't save him," Mary said.

With half-open eyes, he slowly reached for Delilah's arm, "It's okay." He said in a low voice, his breath hitched. The color drained from his face.

"But I don't want you to die. I don't want you to leave me." She cried, her throat thickened with sobs.

He held her hand. "I won't leave you." His breaths slowed, Delilah felt his skin go cold. "I love you, Delilah."

"I love you too." She told him as his grip around her hand loosened as he took his last breath.

Shattered from the grief of losing the only sibling she would ever know, she sobbed over him. A friend, brother, and an innocent life taken at the hands of corrupt witchcraft. Mary gently closed his eyelids, mumbling a short prayer, and wrapped her arms around Delilah, comforting her the best she could. With reddened eyes between sniffles, Delilah noticed the spellbook sitting on the ground near Bryce's mutilated body. She let go of her mother and got up to grab it. Holding it in her hands, a beam of hope shined within her.

"I can bring him back," Delilah said.

Her mother stared at her with furrowed brows. "Delilah, I know you're hurting right now. But there is nothing you can do."

"Yes, there is. I'm a pure-born shifter. With the blood of a pure-born, we can give new life."

"If I'm not mistaken, you can only do that if the shifter is dying. He's already gone. And even if he wasn't, I can't let you do that. You know what happens to shifters who give blood to save a life."

"I know what happens. And it's not too late." Delilah opened the book, flipping through the pages. "I can bring him back, with the revival spell."

CHAPTER 14

Mary gently placed Jackson flat on the ground, as she got up and walked to Delilah. "Baby, I know this is hard, but you've gotta stop. I'm sorry he's gone but you can't do this." She said sternly.

"Why not? The book states that any descendant of Akinde can use the spell."

"On animals! Not humans!"

"Exactly! With this spell, and my pure shifter blood together I can bring him back. And I want to. He saved your life. He deserves this. And you and I both know that Bryce won't be the last one to come after me. It'll never stop, and my powers will just keep getting stronger and harder to control. I'll keep hurting and killing people and I'll never be free." Delilah moved into her mother's arms, hugging her.

Mary held her close. As much as she hated to admit it, she knew her daughter was right. Mary tried so hard to protect Delilah her entire life, but a mother's love and protection could only get her but so far.

"You'll lose your human form forever. " She said.

"I know. But it's worth it. Jackson gets to live again, and I get to be free."

"But I don't want to lose you."

"I'll be around momma. Just, on four legs instead of two."

She and Mary shared a lighthearted laugh. Mary placed her hand on Delilah's chin, wearing a pressed lip smile.

"I'm sorry I never told you about your real father, and no matter how it may have seemed, I never felt any ill ways about you being a shifter. I always knew it made you happier than being a witch, so I understand why you want to do this."

"Thank you, momma. And I forgive you."

Her mother placed a gentle kiss on her forehead before they headed back over to Jackson.

Delilah sat next to him, placing her palm on his cold face. "I'll always be a part of him. We were meant to be forever connected. A piece of my human soul will always live in him."

Delilah held out her hand, placing her index finger in the middle of her palm. "*Kewaa patentibus.*" A small gash formed, blood dripped down her wrist. She gripped Jackson's jaw with her other hand, parting his lips as her blood poured into his mouth. Mary handed her the book, as she held it open, reciting the revival spell as her blood went into him.

"*Na ọgwụ. Novum do vobis vitam.*" She used her finger to smear a line of her blood in the center of his forehead. "With this spell, I give new life."

Delilah placed her hand over his heart as they sat, quietly waiting. After the spell was complete, Jackson would need time to heal. He would be in a comatose state until however long it took for his consciousness to return.

"Take care of him, please. Make sure he gets back home." Delilah said.

"I will." Mary pulled her daughter closer, her arms were like shields of love. As this was the last time she would ever feel the warm embrace of her daughter's skin. "I love you," Mary said to her. Her eyes welled up.

"I love you too, momma," Delilah said.

That's when she felt it. Jackson's chest rose, as his heart began beating. Happiness washed over Delilah as she smiled, breathing a sigh of relief. She looked at her mother, whose look of grief she masked with a smile. Then all at once, Delilah was gone. In her place, was the beast. She rubbed her nose against her mother's lap as she pet her gently. While her daughter's human body was gone, Mary was in a strange way, content. Knowing that Delilah's spirit was still as gleeful and vibrant as she always was. But now, with a sense of freedom that she always wanted.

CHAPTER 15

It had been 48 hours since Mary brought Jackson to Mercy hospital. She made up a story about finding him on the side of the road, unconscious after a car accident. His stab wounds had now healed, but he hadn't awakened yet. She switched rounds with another nurse at the hospital to ensure that she could keep an eye on him and be there when he came to.

As she headed into his room to check his vitals for the day, a woman was sitting in the chair next to his bed. Dark-skinned and dressed in an all-black suit, her hair slicked and pulled back into a tight bun. She sat with her hands on her lap, her eyes on Mary as soon as the door opened. Mary crept in slowly, closing the door behind her. She didn't need to ask the woman who she was. It was only a matter of time before they showed up.

"Is there something I can help you with?" Mary asked.

"I'm sure you already know the answer to that question." The woman got up from her seat, walking towards Mary. "My name is Pamela. I'm from the council, Region three. As you know, our community has an extremely strict code when it comes to violence. Any shifter who commits murder is given death. No exceptions."

"Yes, I'm aware of that," Mary said, straightening her posture and keeping her hands at her sides.

"You know we have ways of keeping a watchful eye on our own. There is nothing that gets past the council. Unfortunately, there are those who mask their scents underground and slip through the cracks. Like Bryce Barbeau and Stephan Reynolds."

"Bryce's family has been looking for him."

"And we'll handle that. As well as Stephan's. But I'm here about your daughter, Delilah." Pamela looked over at Jackson. "And him."

"My daughter is gone. And Jackson won't remember anything. I used a spell to erase his short term memory." She lied. "He only killed to protect himself. As did my daughter. Just like last time. Please, spare them." Mary urged.

"Under the circumstances of this cult business and your daughter giving up her human form, wherever she might be. We've decided that she will face no consequences." Pamela walked over to Jackson's bedside, peering down at him. "And considering Mr. Kinnard here has no memory of this nonsense, according to you. We will spare him as well. For now."

Mary clutched her chest, relieved.

Pamela walked over to Mary, leering at her. "We don't like mess. And we sure as hell don't like to clean up after this witchcraft half-breed nonsense. Word of this cult business must never get out to anyone. Ever. Is that understood?"

Mary nodded. "Yes, understood."

"Good. Hopefully, we won't have to see you again. Goodbye Ms. Simmons."

Pamela left the room. Mary went behind her, closing the door. She leaned against it, her anxiety from the uncertainty of how the council would handle things was finally over. Delilah was safe, roaming around the countryside doing what she loved the most. She could come and go as she pleased, always returning home when she missed the comfort of her mother's love. The only thing left to do now was wait for Jackson to wake up. Whenever that would be.

***

Jackson found himself at the edge of a lake, wearing some kind of traditional Native American clothing. A necklace made of shell, bone, leather, and claw hung from his neck. A mantle made of deerskin draped over his shoulders. He turned around, where his mother Carla and aunt Carrie stood, facing him. Both wearing dresses made of deerskin, with woven hemp belts across their waists. Their eyes, covered in orange and black face paint. There was a small crowd of others standing back in the distance. All wearing similar clothing. He walked towards them, feeling weightless as his mother wrapped her arms around him.

"Mom," He uttered, his eyes flooding with tears.

He turned to Carrie, who welcomed him with open arms. "It's nice to see you again, my nephew."

"I'm so sorry aunt Carrie. I should've protected you." Jackson said.

Carrie smiled, "It's alright. I am where I am meant to be." She brushed her thumb across his chin.

"But you aren't." His mother said. She took his hands into hers. "You have to go back now."

Jackson's forehead creased, "No. I want to stay with you." He pleaded, gripping her hands.

Carla cupped his face with both hands, placing a gentle kiss on his forehead. "It is not your time, my son. But when it is, your family will be waiting." She said.

Carla and Carrie stepped back, as a beam of light covered him. He took in one last look at their graceful faces, before everything went dark, again.

Jackson's eyes opened slowly to a bright light blurring his vision. He lifted his head, peering down at the gown he was wearing, running his fingers across the cotton fabric. Rubbing his eyes, he circled the room. He could hear footsteps from outside the door.

"Hello?" He called out.

The person walking by had stopped, coming inside. "Oh! Mr. Kinnard. You're awake. I'll go let nurse Simmons know." The woman closed the door and kept on down the hall.

He felt a sudden throb of discomfort in his chest, and the memory of being stabbed flashed through him. He looked under his gown where he had been stabbed. Although there were no scars, he could still feel the pressure of the blunt force impaling his flesh. Then the image of Bryce, and blood.... Then Delilah.

"Jackson, you're back!" Mary came through the door with wide eyes. She went over to him, wrapping her arms around him in a hug. "Thank goodness. I was beginning to worry. It's been almost a month."

"What? What are you talking about? Where is she? Where's Delilah?"

Mary's eyes held a haunted look as she bit her lower lip. Her eyes drifted away from him. "She's gone."

Confused, a weight settled on his heart. His head pounded from the trust of a sudden headache. "No. she can't be."

Mary felt that the less he knew, the better. If he thought Delilah was dead, then he could move on and wouldn't go looking for her. As long as they stayed away from each other, he would be safe. After she lied to the council about wiping his memory, she had to ensure that Jackson played his part. It hurt her deeply to lie to him like this, but it was the only way.

"Jackson, you died. She sacrificed herself and used a spell to bring you back." She took a seat at the edge, next to him. "I need you to listen to me, someone from the council came by. They were going to execute you for murdering Stephan. I told them that I wiped your memory and they let you live." She clenched his shoulders. "You must never speak of me, Delilah, or anything that happened here. To anyone, ever. Do you understand?"

He nodded, choking back tears.

"I know it's hard. It is for me too. But this is what she wanted."

His shoulders sagged, "So what am I supposed to do now?"

"Well, a new life is a blessing. You seem like a determined young man, and I know you're compassionate just like she was. I'm sure you'll figure it out. You saved my life, and in a way, you saved hers too." She got up to leave the room. "I got your car from your aunt's place. It's in the parking lot. I'll bring you something for the headache and we'll get you processed for release, and you should be good to go tomorrow." She said before heading out.

Jackson laid back against his pillow, staring up at the light fixtures. The glare stung his eyes, triggering his headache but it was better than having to deal with the pain of losing Delilah. She deserved so much better than this. Better than him. Even though it was her choice to sacrifice herself, he would never forgive himself for not being there to stop her.

He felt like a failure. Now he had no one, and death seemed better than living out the rest of his days stuck in despair and loneliness. Needing a distraction, he reached for the tiny remote on the table tray next to his bed and turned on the TV. He flicked through the channels, looking for anything to temporarily fill the void and block out his thoughts. That's when he came across a news segment where a

poorly drawn sketch of a beast displayed on the
screen.

*"The victim says that the creature who attacked
him and his friends last night was some kind of wolf.
Authorities urge citizens to avoid the area until
further notice. This attack, similar to the killing of a
young boy in Cedar Rapids, Iowa just a few weeks
ago…"*

Feys. Jackson thought. Last night must've been a
full moon, and he knew it had to be someone who
was recently turned. An unfortunate soul who would
be dealt with by the council sooner than later. Then
he remembered what Delilah told him. About wanting
to travel around the country helping feys adjust to the
lifestyle of the beast. This had to be it. His calling.
This is what he was meant to live for. To honor her
life and memory by helping others. And the first stop
on his newfound journey of purpose, was Iowa.

Epilogue
{An intro to River's Moonlight}

October 2017
Three Years Later

The faint cries of what sounded like a young girl emerged from the edge of the woods. The smell of blood was sharp and cut through my nose like a sharp blade. I ran towards the sounds of anguish, the smell of burning human flesh sent my senses into overdrive. As I reached the edge, that's when I saw her. The girl, lying in the grass on the side of the road. The bodies of two mangled adults lay among the car wreckage. I slowly make my way towards the girl, my footsteps slow and steady. As I get closer, she sees me. Her eyes grow wide and her mouth trembles, but she doesn't scream. Glass shards sticking from her skin, she's trembling. I lower my head, my nose grazes her skin as I begin to lick the wounds on her arm. That's when she reaches for me, seemingly no longer afraid. Her brown eyes searching the depths of mine. Into my soul. I don't know who she is, but I know what this means. I'm not done yet…

"Are you finished?"

I look up from my glass, as the bartender stares at me with his hands pressed against the countertop.

"Huh?"

"Are you done with your drink yet? I'm closing in five minutes." The bartender said.

"Uh, yeah." I push the glass away, digging into my pocket as I get up from the stool, but before I head to the door, the news playing on the television behind the bar catches my attention.

"Now to breaking news… two teenagers were attacked tonight in what authorities suspect to be another bear attack. One of the victims, a young man was pronounced dead at the scene. The other victim, a young woman was taken to a local hospital where she is currently fighting for her life-"

The bartender turns off the T.V.

"Wait! Turn that back on." I ask. My heart pounding as dread crept its way inside.

"Didn't you hear me? We're closed. You can watch the news at home." He said, slapping a dishrag over his shoulder as he walked towards the register.

I huffed, pulling the crunched up twenty dollar bill from my pocket and slapping it on the counter. "Have a good night," I say sarcastically as I head to the door.

As I head home, I can't stop thinking about my dream. About the little girl. I had just returned to Chicago two days ago from Virginia. The last stop on my journey around the country. Tracking down feys and helping them get accustomed to their new lives. It was my way of honoring my sister and finding a purpose in my life. And now, three years later, I was home again. But that dream was a sign that my journey wasn't over. And now the news of another attack? I knew this couldn't be a coincidence. And I knew it wasn't a bear that attacked those people. I had to find this survivor before it was too late.

***

I stand huddled in the narrow phone booth, dialing slowly trying to remember the correct number. The pounding in my chest comes back as I wait for her to answer. Hoping, she will answer.

"Hello." She says softly, most likely hesitant due to the unknown number.

"Kayla. Hey… it's me."

I hear her take a short breath. There was a pause before she spoke again. "Jax? It's really you?"

Her voice trembles, and suddenly I regret calling. "Yes. It's been a while. I know." I respond.

"A while? It's been almost three years. I didn't even know if you were alive."

"Well I am, and I'm back in Chicago," I said.

"You're here?" she asks excitedly. "Are you at your cabin? I'll come by later and-"

"Kayla, I need to ask you something. Did you hear about the attack last night?"

She scoffs. "Yeah. What about it?"

"There was a survivor. Has she been identified?"

"I don't know. And I don't care. Why?"

"I need to find her."

She scoffs again. "I don't hear from you for all this time, and this is what you call to talk about? Another girl?"

"Kayla, please…"

"You don't even call to tell us that you're alright. Not once. I've thought about you nearly every day since you left us. I've missed you so much…" Her voice creaks.

I sigh heavily, pressing my eyes closed. I knew it was a bad idea to call.

"Kayla, I'm sorry."

"Whatever Jax. I've gotta go." She sniffled.

She hangs up on me and I slam the phone against the receiver. Fuck. I knew calling Kayla would end like this. But I knew if anyone would have information about the attack, it would be her or her father and brother, but I wasn't ready to talk to either of them. I would just have to find this girl on my own. Before the next full moon.

***

A week had gone by, and all I knew about the survivor of the attack was that her name was River Lewis and that she was seventeen-years-old. Due to her being a minor, the news hadn't released her identity right way. By the time I found the correct hospital, she had already been released. The full moon was last night, and I was too late. I just prayed to God that she hadn't killed anyone. But being her first turn, in a city like this? I knew that was impossible. But the next full moon was 4 weeks away, and I still had time.

As I walked through the park, headed to my cabin that hid in the middle of the woods, that's when I saw it. A body in the distance. I could see dark hair and blood. Judging by the shape, I could tell it was a female. Oh no... I hurried towards the body, looking around to make sure no one else was around. It was 6 am, so the park was empty. As I approached the body, nude, and covered in blood. I knelt, checking for a pulse. She was alive. And her scent was unmistakable. A shifter. I looked over at her back and saw the scars. It had to be her. I quickly lifted her into my arms and headed into the woods. When I got far enough away from the edge of the park, I laid her down near a tree. I took off my jacket and placed it over her. I didn't want to leave her like this, but the walk to my cabin was too far and I needed to call someone for help. There was a payphone across the street from the park. I dashed over and swiftly called the only person that I knew who would help.

"Kayla. It's me again. I need you…"

"Jax? What is it now? I told you I don't know anything about that girl." Kayla said, annoyed.

"I found her."

"You what?"

"I found her. In the woods. She turned last night and she's in bad shape. I need you to come to my cabin. And bring spare clothes. Please."

"Are you kidding me! I want nothing to do with this!"

"Kayla, please! If I take her to my cabin alone, she'll be terrified. But if you're there I can maybe talk to her without her freaking out."

Kayla mumbled curses to herself, huffing in agitation. "Why should I even help you?" she said.

"Because you've always had my back… and I miss you."

"Okay. I'll come." She said.

"Thanks, Kayla. I mean it." I hung up the phone and ran back to the park to get River.

When I reached the spot, she was still, there. Still unconscious. Thank God. I picked her up and made my way to my cabin, hoping that Kayla would actually come. I walked with slow steps, so he wouldn't wake her. When I arrived, I placed her down on the floor, a few feet away from the fireplace. I lit it to keep her warm before going to his bedroom to get a blanket. I took a seat on his sofa, slouching, and taking a deep breath. I looked at her, laying there. Wondering what I would say, how I would explain all of this, what she had become. It was easier with the other feys I met and helped while traveling. They were mostly older. But this girl was only seventeen. Hopefully being around the same age was an advantage. Maybe she would take to me and Kayla better that way. Whatever happened, I just hoped that she would be okay. And hoped to God that she wouldn't wake up before Kayla arrived.

To be continued...

The journey is just beginning ...

*Check out the rest of
The Moonlight Series*

Available Now!

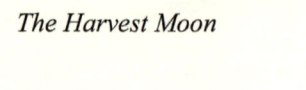

The Harvest Moon

ABOUT THE AUTHOR

Born and raised in the Washington D.C. area, writing has been a passion of mine since I was young. I started writing my first book, 'My Colorblind Rainbow' in 2013. In 2017, I decided to continue writing, taking a leap of faith and following my dreams of publishing my first book which made the 'In the Margins Award Long List' for YA fiction 2018. I launched **Hardy Publications** in September of 2017, working as a freelance ghostwriter, author, and literary blogger. I also use my platform to raise awareness for different charities and non-profit organizations, donating a portion of my book royalties to help others in need.

The Harvest Moon

www.ingramcontent.com/pod-product-compliance
Lightning Source LLC
Chambersburg PA
CBHW022023170626
46808CB00003B/1031